TALES OF A SECURITY GUARD

Boris Bacic

Dedicated to everyone who supported me and believed in my talent (that means you, stranger on the internet). If you've read my stories online before and still decided to buy my book, that means you want to support my work and I appreciate it a ton.

TABLE OF CONTENTS

Introduction

Back when I was 20 years old, I started working for a security company, whose job was to protect various households and business buildings via alarm systems, surveillance cameras, etc. My own duty encompassed patrolling around the office parking lot, where our HQ was. In case of an alarm, I was to drive out to the scene and assess whether there's been a burglary and if necessary, apprehend the burglar or call the police (most likely the latter though, as we were unarmed). I stayed with the company for almost two years before I quit, due to the low pay and horrible work-life balance. Years later, I'd run into various stories on Nosleep, which spurred my imagination to life and woke up the author in me, which had been asleep for years prior to that. The Search and Rescue Officer stories were the ones that really managed to grip me with fear and terror while I read them and all of a sudden I got this idea – what if I made my own story, but from the perspective of a security guard?
I wanted to illicit the same reaction in my readers, which the writer of the SaR stories evoked in me, however I had no concrete ideas. I brainstormed for a bit on and off and eventually just decided that I had to put it on paper, so I managed to cook one part of the series up, literally conjuring it out of thin air in one afternoon, not expecting any response when I posted it online.

You can imagine my surprise when I saw the post exploding with comments and upvotes, asking for more parts. As of today, the *I work as a security guard for a company that takes jobs no one else will* series on Nosleep has more than 10 successful parts and is nowhere near being finished. The really good thing about the series was the fact that it gave me the freedom to work on and off on it, without full commitment, like other stories. I could write 5 parts, take a break and come back with more parts later. The series has grown so much in popularity, that I decided to publish it as a book, so that all who have enjoyed the stories can have it memorialized. You, the readers, are who I have to thank the most, because without your support and encouragement, none of this would be possible.

Thank you for your continued support and remember always:

NEVER, EVER GO OFF TRAIL.

NIGHT GUARD

Phase 1

When I first saw the ad, I didn't think twice.
Earn up to 80$ per night with our simple job as a night guard. No prior experience required.
The ad said and I submitted my resume as fast as I could, fearing it could disappear or be taken by someone else at any moment. Not two hours after submitting my application, I got a response on my email that I've been hired and can start working from tonight.
It struck me as odd that there was no job interview and that I needed to start working right away, but hey, maybe they urgently needed someone. I've been jobless for over a year now, so I naively ignored any red flags and was just happy to have a job.
I went to the given address at 8 pm and it turned out to be an office building.
"Hello?" I called out when I entered, but no one responded.
The hall I was in was engulfed in darkness and the only source of light was coming through the pane of glass on the door which had the name SECURITY on it. I knocked on the door, but there was no response. I decided to open it and sure enough, it was empty. On the desk was a note, left clear as day for me to read. It said:

To the new night guard,

Your shift starts at 8:04 pm and ends at 4:04 am. When you arrive to the building and relieve the other guard of duty, you can stay in the security room as long as you want, but you have to use the elevator to get to the top floor once at any time during the shift. Once up there, you have to proceed to the end of the attic and flip the switch on the wall. That's it.

If the other guard is not in the security room at the time of your arrival, make a report in the notebook and we will inform his family.

As for your duty:

It's very likely that when you push the top floor button (25), the elevator will go past that floor and you may see that it stopped on floor 33. If this happens, do not try pushing any of the buttons, since they will not work.

Go forward through the hallway. Note that the flashlight may not do much to illuminate the area, but still bring it with you (there's a spare in the drawer). Some people report hearing or seeing office employees working at their desks, coming from any of the adjacent rooms. You may see them doing something like typing on a computer which isn't turned on, or typing one word over and over on the screen. Ignore them at all costs. It is currently unknown if the employees are real or a manifestation of the mind, but ignoring them should keep you safe. Turn left when you reach the end of the hallway. You may sometimes see a man standing in the middle, blocking your way. He will do you no harm, so long as you maintain eye contact with him. You have to get past him, so put your hand on the wall to your right (or left) and slide it across as you go through to avoid stumbling and losing eye contact with the man.

He will keep following you with his gaze and try to distract you. Reports indicate he may point behind you with a look of fear on his face to try to get you to look away. You may also hear loud crashing sounds or voices right next to you, but ignore them.

Once you reach the end of the hall and round the corner (and not a moment sooner!), you're safe from the individual. When you reach the exit which leads to the staircase, proceed down. Make sure to note what floor you are on and if any of the floors start repeating on your way down, immediately go back up to floor 33 and then start descending again.

If you see any of the other stair doors open, proceed carefully, especially focusing on the ceiling (or underside of the stairs). You may start to hear footsteps coinciding with your own behind you. Don't stop to listen and don't turn around, just proceed as you normally would. If you feel that the footsteps are getting closer, go faster, but try not to arouse suspicion.

If you hear a high-pitched scream coming from above (it usually sounds like a mountain lion), run down to floor 25 as fast as you can and pray you are faster than the thing chasing you .

If you are forced to continue going down despite the floors repeating, enter the closest floor. You will find yourself back in the hallway of floor 33, so simply repeat the steps from before.

Once you reach floor 25, you are in the clear. First, call the elevator and jam the door to keep it open. Press the floor 1 button and go back to the switch. After flipping the switch, the lights will go out. At this point, you will start to hear screams all around you, similar to the one described before. Run to the elevator as fast as you can and enter it, while unjamming the door.

If you did everything right, you should have at least five extra seconds to close the elevator before the entities of the building reach you.

You should be back on the first floor of the security room once the elevator stops. You may spend the rest of the shift however you desire, so long as you don't leave the property between 8:04 pm and 4:04 am. Note that leaving the building at any given moment between the mentioned times will put you back on floor 33. Also note that not flipping the switch before 4:04 am will result in you not being able to leave the building.

Thank you for performing your duties!
Management

It's 1:24 am right now and the elevator doors just opened on their own.

Phase 2

I barely made through the building and it was mentally agonizing beyond words.

At 2 am I entered the elevator, which had been opened for almost an hour prior to that. I took the note with me and followed all the rules written there. The elevator stopped on floor 33 despite my hopes. There was the sound of typing to my left and when I peeked through the shattered glass I saw a guy in formal attire sitting by an old PC layered with dust (which wasn't even turned on) and typing away vigorously. He'd even glance over his shoulder and call out to his imaginary (or invisible) coworkers, saying things like: 'Cindy, do you have that report ready?' or 'The client said we should meet at 2 pm.' I tried not to look at him as I tip-toed through the hallway and turned left. A tall man in a coat stood in front of me and he was staring right at me. I knew I had to maintain eye contact with him, so I slowly went past him. The entire time he tried to distract me by pretending he was about to hit me and hoping I would flinch, pointing to things behind me in a very convincing manner with a look of horror on his face, etc. I swear at one point someone even screamed 'watch out' right in my ear.

Luckily I made it unscathed and going down the stairs to floor 25 was uneventful. I made it to the end of hallway on 25, flipped the switch and rushed back to the elevator as blood-curdling screams echoed all around me. The elevator doors closed just in time for me to hear something heavy slam into it at full force. Luckily, the elevator started descending and the screams slowly faded.

It stopped on floor 1, but the door wouldn't open. I pressed the open button in vain and then… the elevator started moving down. I slammed the number 1 button over and over, but the elevator failed to respond. It went down for an impossible amount of time, descending by my estimation at least 15-20 floors down. And then it finally stopped and the doors opened. In front of me was some kind of a waiting room, with a sofa and lamp table next to it. There was a door opposite of the elevator.

I pressed the buttons over and over, but there was no response. It was clear the elevator wanted me to step out on this floor. Sure enough, as soon as I did, the doors closed again and the elevator went back up. I cursed, frustrated and scared shitless.

I inspected the room and just then realized there was a hastily written note on the lamp table. I picked it up. Here's what it said:

If you're reading this, that means you fell for their trap, just like me. The good news is you made it through the first task on floor 25. The bad news is there is no job and you aren't gonna get paid. Whoever these guys are, they're running some fucking experiments on us like some lab rats. We need to get the fuck out and get to the police.

Read this next part carefully, because your life will depend on it. When you go through the door on your left, you'll find yourself in a mansion of some sorts. You need to make it to the third floor, but it won't be easy. Follow these rules:

FLOOR 1

Go through the hallway, but whatever you do, don't fucking look in the mirror to your left. You may see with your peripheral vision the reflection not mimicking your own movement or just facing and staring at you, but DO NOT look at it. Close your eyes if you have to.

Once you're past the mirror, turn left and go straight. You may hear the toilet flush in the bathroom to your right at this point. If this happens, hide immediately. There's a closet close by. Hide inside and don't make a sound until the old man comes out of the bathroom and is gone. Wait at least one full minute before going out.

Once you're in the clear, climb the stairs in the main hall to the second floor.

FLOOR 2

Turn right and take the second door to the left (blue door). I have no idea what will happen if you take the other doors or turn left. Once through the blue door, you'll find yourself in a big room full of mannequins. Dozens of mannequins will be on both sides. You may hear giggling, and some of them changing the direction of their gazes and their positions or poses when you don't look, but I think they won't harm you if you don't disturb them.

If any of the mannequins' heads drop to the floor and roll in front of you, run as fast as you can and close the door behind you once you're out. You should be close to the stairs again now. Follow the hall how it winds and don't worry about any voices you hear from the adjacent rooms, even if they beg you to come help them. If you hear or see any of the doors opening, hide again. The old man might seem like someone you can overpower easily, but don't even fucking think about it. Once he's gone, climb the stairs.

FLOOR 3

Remember that man from floor 33 who you had to keep eye contact with? He might be here again, but he's gonna be more aggressive this time. You're gonna hear someone scream something like 'I got you now!' right behind you, but ignore it! You will also start to feel a stinging and burning sensation in your eyes. Do your best not to blink. If you have to blink, try not to keep your eyes closed for more than a second. Maintain eye contact with him and go through the hall until you can turn left (left from the original position! That means your right as you're facing the man backwards).

If you see a woman in patient's gowns standing in front of the elevator, facing away from you, just stand next to her and wait for the elevator. If she asks you to come inside the elevator with her, politely decline. If she doesn't say anything, you can step inside with her, but don't talk to her, just stare in front of yourself.

Once you're in the elevator, you'll see that there are no buttons inside. The elevator will start going up on its own. When the elevator stops, wait until the woman steps out and stay inside until the elevator starts moving again. If she asks you if you'll come with her, politely decline again. Once the door closes, the elevator should go up a few more floors. Now if the woman was not there at all, but then you took the elevator and she enters when the doors open, exit immediately. I don't know where you will be and I have no idea what you need to do there, so you're on your own. Hope you don't run into her.

I came back to give you this warning, compiled from my own and other peoples' experiences, so chances are I either made it out or I'm dead somewhere along the way.

If you manage to get out, expose these fuckers and don't let anyone else get fucked over.

Good luck,

Guard who came before you.

You've gotta be fucking kidding me, was my first thought. Ten minutes later though, I was in the clear and managed to get to the elevator by following every rule the guard laid out. I was lucky though. Aside from the old man in the bathroom, no one else bothered me. I heard a giggle and a set of footsteps in the mannequin room, but neither the staring man nor the patient woman were present, so I managed to safely take the elevator, my heart thumping the entire time so fast I thought it was going to burst out of my chest.

The elevator started going up and I prayed I would be back at the reception. My hope was short-lived though, because when the elevator stopped and the doors opened, I was in an advanced security room with a bunch of camera feeds across the entire wall. On the desk on top of the keyboard was another note.

Phase 3

I sat at the desk in front of the camera screens, because I felt like I really needed some respite after the ordeal from before. I was so tired and scared. On the one hand I felt really vulnerable without a weapon, but on the other hand I was glad I didn't have anything that I could potentially use to end myself. I tried not to think about the fact that suicide could prevent a far worse fate.

I glanced at the camera feed. It seemed to be covering some sort of run-down hospital. No one was on any of the cameras, except for one. That patient lady which the guard mentioned in his note was peeking around the corner of one of the cameras, as if she was waiting for someone to walk by to give them a jump-scare. I looked down at the note in front of me. It said:

Still alive? Good.
You're gonna need to follow an even stricter set of rules in order to get past this area, especially making sure you do things according to specific times. First off, no matter when you enter the room, the alarm clock on the desk is going to say 3:19 am.

I glanced at the small clock in front of me. 3:19 am and it just turned to 3:20. I continued reading.

You need to follow these rules according to the times and NOT be late nor early anywhere, this is the most important part.

First off, take a look at all the cameras and see if the staring man is anywhere on them. If he is, you'll see him staring directly at the camera. Turn off the camera and then turn it back on again. The man should be gone. If he's not, repeat until he is.

Take some time to rest and prepare. At exactly 3:35 am, go out and conduct a patrol around the building as if you were on regular guard duty. You need to check every room on floors 1 and 2 and you need to be back in the security room by 4:00 am.

While you're patrolling, you may see a doctor in one of the rooms. He usually just appears out of nowhere, the room is empty the one moment and then you turn around and he's there, performing surgery on a mangled corpse. If you see him, back away slowly and try to exit the room without being noticed. If he calls after you, don't ignore him. He'll ask you to assist him by giving him surgical tools from the tray, so just do what he asks. Try not to give him the wrong tools, otherwise you might be the one he's going to dissect on that table next.

You probably saw the woman peeking behind the corner on the camera by now. Don't worry, she'll be gone during your patrol.

Once you are done with your patrol, get back to the camera room. You may sometimes see another guard sitting by the desk when you return. You can talk to him normally like you would to a friend or coworker. Do not try to talk to him about your current predicament. At 4:15 he'll say he needs to conduct a patrol and as soon as he leaves the room, lock the door behind him.

From 4:15 to 4:30 you may hear knocking on the door and rattling of the knob, but you'll see no one on the camera covering the outside of the security room. Ignore the knocking and rattling, no matter how incessant it becomes. Even if you hear desperate cries for help in the voices of women or children or the guard from before, don't open the door. They can't get inside if you don't let them in, so you should be safe.

4:30 – 4:40 you have a break, so take a moment to recuperate. Do not take a nap!

From 4:40 am you should focus on the cameras. You will start to feel really sleepy. No matter what you do, you must not fall asleep. As you get sleepier, you will also start to notice movement in your peripheral vision or start to feel like someone is in the room with you, standing right over your shoulder and breathing. Just focus on the cameras, no matter how vivid the presence becomes.

At 5:00 am, if you hear raspy breathing coming from the ceiling, DO NOT LOOK UP! Close your eyes and count to 10. You will feel cold fingers touching you and the raspy breathing will be in your ear, but whatever you do, keep your eyes closed until it all stops completely. Continue focusing on the cameras until 5:29, but do not leave the security room under any circumstances.

*At exactly 5:29 am, get ready to move quickly. As
soon as the clock ticks 5:30 am (and not a second
sooner!), unlock and open the door and run for it.
Just run straight into the elevator at the end of the
hallway and ignore the growling behind you. Don't
look behind, because you need every second here. The
elevator door will be open and it will automatically
close and take you out of there once you're in.
I'll be waiting on the other side. Good luck, brother.
Guard who came before you.*

I placed down the note and exhaled sharply. It was
3:24 am. I glanced at the cameras. The staring man
was on one of the feeds. I restarted it and sure
enough, in less than a second while the camera was
off he just disappeared.
At 3:35 am I went outside, conducting my patrol
carefully, but still doing my best to hurry up. I
glanced at my watch every minute or so.
As I finished the last room and was about to exit, I
heard someone humming behind me. I turned around
and saw a surgeon in blood-stained clothes dissecting
a corpse on the table which was not previously there.
I froze, but the doc was transfixed on the 'surgery',
humming more violently as he sawed through one of
the corpse's arms.
Seeing this broke me out of my trance and I slowly
backed away, reaching for the door. As I turned
around to face the exit, I stopped dead in my tracks.
"Ah-ah!" The doc exclaimed and I turned around, my
heart ready to explode.
"Almost forgot to take care of this." He grabbed a
scalpel and continued cutting the corpse, paying no
attention to me.

I silently exhaled in relief and left the place slowly. As soon as I was at a safe distance, I sprinted back to the security room. The room was empty, no guard in there like the note mentioned.

I locked the door and continued following the agonizing rules on the list until 5:29 am, ignoring anything else in the room until then. As soon as the clock ticked 5:30, I heard a growl behind me. I opened the door and ran faster than I ever knew possible, while the growl turned into something that sounded like demonic barking. It kept getting closer and closer.

I ran into the elevator, practically ramming the backside with my shoulder. I turned around just in time to see a pair of red eyes staring at me from the hallway before the elevator door closed.

The elevator started going up and stopped shortly after. When it opened, I found myself in an empty white room with an electronic door on the other side. The only two things that contrasted the white walls and floor were a monitor mounted on one of the walls and the silhouette of a person in a dark uniform. He had the sign which said SECURITY on the back.

"I finally found you!" I smiled and stepped out of the elevator, relieved.

The guard looked at me with a confused expression, so I tried to explain who I was and thanked him for leaving the instructions behind for me. He shook his head:

"What are you talking about?" He asked.

"You said in your note that you'd be waiting on the other side." I said.

"What note? Look bro, I'm just trying to find my way out of here. Been trying to find a way to open this door for ages." He looked even more confused by this point.

"Look man, I've been following these notes you left, because you said you'd be here, so just cut the bullshit." I took out the note and presented it to him. He inspected it with a serious look on his face and then looked at me and said:

"Afraid you got the wrong guy, bro. This isn't my handwriting."

"Well if it wasn't you, who was it then?" I angrily remarked.

Just then, the monitor on the wall turned on and a message flashed across the screen.

Phase 4

WELCOME, NEW RECRUITS.
The message on the monitor displayed before disappearing. A new message replaced it and the guard and I had to get closer to read what the wall of text said.

You've done well so far. You're not far from reaching your goal, but know that your tasks will get harder from here on out and you will have to work as a team to survive.

The door will open in 1 minute. You will see a guardhouse to your left. Enter it and read the note.

As soon as we were done reading, the monitor turned off and the electronic door opened with a loud hum. A cold gust of air hit me in the face instantly and as we stepped through the door, I realized we were outside in some sort of park.

"What the fuck?" The other guard said – "Hey, maybe we can just run for it. I mean, fuck their rules, right?"

I shook my head:

"Gotta be a catch. They wouldn't just let us leave. This probably isn't even real. Let's check the guardhouse, first."

We went inside the guardhouse, which had a desk and chair inside. The note was on top of the desk next to a clock which read 00:05. The note said:

Out of all the rules there are three main ones you need to strictly follow at all times. The first rule is never, EVER go off trail. If you do, getting lost will be the least of your troubles.

Never stay together for too long, because it attracts them more easily to you. That is the second rule. Ending with the first two rules, the third rule is, whenever the guards reunite, they should use code phrases (example: guard 1 asks 'where does the cat go?' and guard 2 answers 'to the alley'. Note that the code must be recited exactly how it is agreed upon, word by word.)

Moving on to the rest of the rules, one guard should stay in the guardhouse, while the other patrols around the park (patrols take about 10 minutes). For the guard patrolling:

Under no circumstances is the guard allowed to leave the trail when patrolling (see rule 1). Turn left at the crossroads and you will come back full circle back at the guardhouse. If you happen to hear the other guard's voice coming from the trees, calling for help, ignore it. You will hear his voice on a loop, usually repeating the same phrase with the same intonation over and over. Pay attention to the sounds of animal life, too. If the park suddenly gets quiet, finish your patrol normally, but do not look behind or glance at the trees. During your patrol, every 5 minutes or so, loudly shout a simple word like 'hello' into the air. If your voice doesn't echo, run back to the guardhouse immediately.

Should you see a hiker in the middle of the trail, keep the flashlight pointed at his face at all times. He will ask you to move it away, stating it's too bright, but don't listen to him. He will also tell you he understands your situation and will tell you to follow him since he knows a way out. Decline his offer. After this, he should leave. Do not take the light off him until he steps off the trail. For the guard in the guardhouse:

To stay safe, keep the door and window firmly shut at all times, save for when the patrolling guard comes back. It may get annoyingly hot inside, but do not open anything. You may take off your jacket or shirt to alleviate the discomfort.

Do not pay attention to any tapping on the windows. If you hear or see droplets falling on the desk in front of you, slowly stand up and leave the guardhouse. Stay outside for 2-3 minutes and the droplets should be gone when you go back inside. If they are still there, exit again and wait for another 2-3 minutes. When the patrolling guard returns, ask him the code question while avoiding eye contact. If he doesn't respond or responds incorrectly, exit the guardhouse while avoiding eye contact and then return inside. The fake guard will be gone.

If you survive until 1:00 am, both guards should proceed together to the end of the trail and turn right at the crossroads (do not do this before 1:00 am). At this point, the forest life will be completely quiet and the only sound surrounding you will be occasional hurried footsteps coming off the trail. They can only approach you in the dark, so do your best to train your flashlights on them, even if you can't see them clearly. The guards should split to cover both sides with light.

End your task by reaching the end of the trail with a gate. That is your exit point (make sure to take this note with you, you will need it).

"Dammit." The other guard said and we sat in silence for a moment.

I scratched my cheek and said:

"Alright, I'll take the first patrol. What should our code be?"

He thought for a moment and then said:

"Shit man, I dunno. How about this? I'll ask 'What should these fuckers do?' And you can say 'let us go'."

"You got it. What's your name, by the way?" I asked. The guard said his name was Sam and I introduced myself, as well. I left for the patrol with the flashlight and stuck strictly to the trail. Nothing major happened, no sounds off the trail, etc, but I did run into the hiker mentioned in the note. He seemed friendly and all, but I followed the rules and kept the beam pointed in his face, declining everything he asked.

Eventually he left and I finished my patrol and returned to the guardhouse. After we confirmed the codes, Sam left for his own patrol. I followed the set of rules until he came back, confirming the code with him. By the time I finished my second patrol, it was 01:03 am and it was time to go. We quietly walked the trail, focusing on our footsteps and the deafening silence around us. And then the footsteps off the trail started.

It sounded like someone was frantically running from one tree to another, stopping for a few seconds in between. This recurred over and over as Sam and I did our best to focus our beams on the source of the sound, but no matter how quick our reactions were, we never seemed to be able to catch whoever ran there. I caught a glimpse of a nude, emaciated man or woman here and there, but they always seemed to be just out of reach, either hiding behind a tree the moment I shone my light or disappearing into the dark altogether.

Finally, Sam and I reached the end of the trail and entered a fenced area with a gate on the other side. There was a pedestal in the middle and an object on top of it. When we approached it, it became clear it was a gun, with a note under it.

Sam took the note and read it aloud:

"Read the first letter of each paragraph of the previous note."

We both looked at the note and read the letters silently together. And then as the realization hit us, we scrambled for the gun. After a moment of wrestling, the gun was in my hand and I held it pointed at Sam.

"Don't do this, man. I have a wife and young daughter, please." He begged.

I held my finger on the trigger, intermittently looking at him and the gate. I had to get out of here. I've had enough of this bullshit. I looked at Sam's pleading face one more time. A moment later I lowered and then dropped the gun on the ground and said:

"I'm not gonna play their game. I won't become a killer for their entertainment. We can find a different way out, I'm sure."

I went towards the gate to inspect it and then heard Sam's voice behind me:

"I'm sorry, man."

I turned around and saw him pointing the gun at me.

"What are you doing, Sam?"

"You read the note, man. One must die. There's no other way."

"Put the gun down, dammit. We can both make it out of here alive. We just gotta work together." I didn't believe my own words, but I'd be damned if I'd murder another human being for these sick bastards' entertainment.

"I'm sorry. I have to get back to my family." Sam said.

"Sam, no!"

He pulled the trigger, but the bang never came. Instead, there was a click and Sam dropped the gun, holding his hand in pain.

"What the fuck, something just pricked me!" Sam shouted.

He and I stared at each other and then all of a sudden, Sam's eyes rolled behind his eyelids and he fell on the ground, convulsing and frothing at the mouth. I ran over to help him, but I didn't know what to do. He stopped moving completely a moment later and his eyes closed, as his breathing stopped along with the movement. I shook him and called his name, but it was too late. He was already dead.

Just then, the gate started to open.

Phase 5

I knew I couldn't afford to waste any more time, so I went through the gate, leaving Sam's body behind. I listened as the gate closed and the ground beneath my feet started moving. Then the lights came on and I realized I was in a big elevator which started descending. Part of me had somehow come to terms with the fact that I was probably going to die here, but for some reason when you're in a situation where your life is at stake and you desperately want to get out by any means necessary, your body and brain defy your wish to give up and pushes you to fight on. The elevator stopped and the gated door opened, revealing a damp, dark room in front of me. There was a little cart next to the door on the other side. A folder lay on top of the cart. A circular logo with the name 'THE COMPANY' was on the front. Below was the motto 'Your safety is our success'.

When I opened the folder, I saw Sam's face. It was his file. In it I saw everything about him, including age, family and even behavioral patterns observed by these freaks. And then the next page was my file. They knew everything about me. Not just my age, nationality, etc., but also my ways of thinking and everything I have been through during the test so far. They had predictions about my behavior before I even did something. They knew my every move. The last page underneath my file was a note. Here's what it said:

Congratulations on surviving this far!

You have only one last task to complete before you earn your reward, which is to reach the elevator on the other side of this area. The list of rules for the final part is as follows:

Once you are through this door, proceed straight through the corridor. Do not look, get close or touch the glass on the left and right side, despite the irresistible urge. Don't stop for longer than two seconds at a time. During the entire time, you will hear whispers coming from the other side of the glass. If the whispers suddenly stop, run as fast as you can to the door.

Once you reach the door, you will find yourself outside on a wide bridge. There will be one person aimlessly wandering there. He may look weak and drunk, but don't underestimate him. Only move when he is not looking at you. When he faces you, stand as still as you can. If you see him stop all movement suddenly and go silent, he may have sensed you. The best thing to do is to stand still and not breathe. He may approach and inspect you, but do not move a muscle until you see him calmed down and facing away.

Do not even think about making a break for the door when you're close to it and him being a distance away. If he sees you, he will catch you no matter how close to the door you are.

Close the door behind you and you will find yourself in a dormitory. You will see pebbles on a wooden plate next to you. Put them in your pocket and make sure to always have at least one ready in your hand. Proceed through the next area as quietly as possible, especially if you hear footsteps and sniffing close by (be especially aware of creaking floorboards). If you assume you may have attracted its attention, toss the pebbles at a distance to distract it (do not run while it is distracted). Do not go for the exit yet, as the creature is standing in your way.

Look for room 109. By this point the creature will most likely be aware of your presence, so get inside the room and lock it as fast as possible. You will see that there is nowhere to hide, since the room is empty. That's not a problem, since the creature is blind. Run to any corner of the room and stay there as quietly as you can. Try to remain calm as the creature screams and rams the door.

Once it is inside, it will inspect the room and sniff the air. You'll be safe as long as you make no sound. After a minute or so, the creature will leave and you will be able to get to the next exit safely. Exit the dormitory through the back door and close it. When you turn left you will see-

The rest of the note was unintelligible, save for a few words and the signature 'The Company' below. I narrowed my eyes, scanning the page over and over, but no matter how many times I read it, the text remained the same. I cursed loudly and put the page in my pocket, inhaling and exhaling deeply. Final stretch. No matter what happens after this, it would be over and I knew it.

I opened the door and as soon as I did, the whispers came from both sides. It sounded unnatural, as if whoever was on the other side of the glass was mocking me with their friends behind my back and trying to be quiet, but failing. I proceeded for a whole minute before they suddenly stopped. And then loud slamming on both sides of the glass started. Handprints started to appear on the glass. First one, then two, then ten, a hundred, a thousand, all within the span of ten seconds or so.

I sprinted across the corridor and rammed the door with my shoulder. I turned around to close it, but the corridor was calm again. No sounds and no handprints. I took no chances and I closed the door behind me.

I turned back and faced the sight before me. I was on a wide metallic bridge in the middle of nowhere. There were street lights on it, illuminating the entirety of the area. A very frail-looking person stood in the middle of the bridge, hunched forward and looking like he could barely hold his weight on his own legs. I couldn't see below the bridge, because it was too dark, but I was definitely somewhere that looked like outside.

Slowly, I started to cross the bridge, making sure to stop whenever the person on the bridge looked in my direction. He seemed completely oblivious to my presence when I stood still, since he cut in front of me a few times without even looking in my direction. It wasn't until I was close enough that I could hear the wheezing sounds coming from the person, as if he had difficulty breathing. Could he really overpower me?

Nevertheless, I carefully crossed the bridge and closed the door. As soon as I entered the dorm, I took the pebbles and perked up my ears. No sounds yet. Hastily, I found room 109 and as soon as my hand touched the doorknob, a blood-curdling scream echoed throughout the hallway. I quickly entered and locked the door and then rushed to the corner, standing as still as possible, doing my best to steady my breathing.

The door started to rattle violently as whatever was on the other end rammed it over and over. I could see with my peripheral vision that the door was about to give way and soon enough, it fell straight from the hinges. A naked, skinny-looking creature with no eyes and a sharp row of teeth burst inside, jerking its head in all directions, looking for me. It then started to intermittently sniff the air and stop to listen.

I had to clasp my hands over my mouth to stop myself from whimpering. Soon enough, the creature left the room. I waited for a whole minute before peeking out into the corner, still scared shitless. No one was there, so I proceeded to find the exit. After opening the back door, I found myself in another hallway. I turned left and braced myself, ready to face whatever was there. In front of me at the end of the hall was an elevator. But between me and elevator stood none other than the staring man.

Our eyes locked and I knew what I had to do. I heard screams in my ears and felt things brushing against me from behind and touching my neck and face, but I didn't take my eyes off him. I hurried up to the elevator, and it opened on its own. I entered and continued staring at the man and just before the door closed, something unexpected happened.

The man nodded and looked away.

The elevator started ascending this time. I had no idea where it was going to take me, but before I could process that thought properly, it opened again. In front of me was a room engulfed in darkness and only a small beam of light shone in the distance ahead. Hesitantly, I stepped out of the elevator and started walking towards the light. And then more lights turned on from the ceiling, blinding me for a moment and illuminating the entire room.

"Excellent work." A voice in front of me said.

It didn't take me long to realize that I was in some sort of control room and the voice was coming in front of me, from the place where the beam of light had previously been. There was a big rotating chair there and whoever was talking was facing away from me, so I couldn't see them.

"You have successfully completed your assignment." The voice said again.

"Who the hell are you? What do you want from me?!" I shouted.

The chair swung around and a man in a suit revealed to be sitting in it.

"To congratulate you." He said "I usually don't like to go out on the field, but this is a special opportunity."

Anger started to boil in me when I saw how nonchalant he was about this whole situation. I started to stride towards him, but then heard the distinctive sound of a gun being cocked behind my head.

"It's okay, Sam." The man said.

I turned around to look at my assailant. It was Sam, the security guard, alive and well.

"Sam?" I asked "I watched you die. What the hell is this?"

"Sam is an amazing actor. I'm starting to think he should've gone for a different career." The man in the chair said.

"You were in on this the whole time? I don't believe this." I asked and then faced the man in the chair again " Well your test is complete, right? Time to kill me?"

The man threw his head back in laughter and said: "Kill you? Don't be silly. This was necessary for evaluation. We have to go through a very strict hiring process, because we hire only the most suitable candidates. I know the test was stressful, but you passed with flying colors! Forget that whole 80$ per shift thing. The money we'll be paying you will cover all your debts, medical bills and then some."

I let out a chuckle at the absurdity of the situation and said:

"Hiring process? This was what, some kind of job orientation the entire time?"

"Well… yes. What our company deals with here is not ordinary guard duty, as you saw back there. And this is why we need to make sure our candidates don't do something to endanger themselves… or others."

"So all those things back there? They weren't real?" I asked.

"Oh they're as real as they come. And you were in actual danger the whole time. We have intervention units always ready, but sometimes... accidents do happen. This is the process candidates are subjected to. And out of 43 applicants, you were the only one to make it to the end!"

"So you want me to work for you?" I looked at Sam, who had a neutral expression on his face and then back at the man "What if I refuse?"

"Then you get a slightly higher compensation than was mentioned in the ad for your shift and you go home and look for another job." The man shrugged.

"I could go to the police and rat you out." I replied.

"You could. You could tell them everything. But you'd find that the police found no trace of anything you mentioned. No ghosts, no monsters. Not even an ad listed by any company you mentioned. In fact the company itself is not registered anywhere. There's nothing, except an old abandoned building."

He motioned for someone on the side to come. A woman approached me with a paper and pen. She handed them to me. At just one glance I realized it was a contract for the company as a security guard and the compensation was shocking, to say the least. The amount they paid would cover all my bills and I could finally move out of the shithole I live in now. The man continued:

"You could walk away and go to the police. Or you could work for us. Help the world and the vulnerable residents by keeping them safe from the horrors you witnessed. Because their safety is our success." He smiled.

I frantically clicked the pen over and over, looking at the man's smug face and then at Sam. He nodded subtly to me as I looked at the contract once more. So much money...

Before I could change my mind, I signed it and handed it back to the lady. The man smiled widely and then stood up and shook my hand, as he said:

"Welcome to The Company."

SECURITY GUARD

Introduction to the job
I've been a security guard in my company for over two years now, but the work my company does is not your typical run-of-the-mill. To put it simply, my company accepts jobs which no other security company will. That includes high-risk assignments which often result in deaths of the staff members or abandoning their posts.

Let me take it from the top.

Initial rules

When I started working here, they had a very long meeting with me to explain all the potential dangers I would be facing. They also made me sign an NDA and a bunch of other papers which stated that if something were to happen to me, the company would not be held responsible.

They explained that the job is risky, but also paid well. I had been jobless for a while and jumped at the opportunity regardless of the risks. Unlike most other companies though, they made me read through the entire NDA aloud and made sure I was aware of all the rules. Some of the things I read there made me think initially that this was all a joke. But then I saw that my superior was dead serious.

My job would basically be to provide support to the guards at other posts via comms and patrol the perimeter I was stationed at. Now our HQ was located in an office building compound which had multiple companies renting the adjacent buildings. I would mostly work nights with the occasional mornings. The rules were as follows:

I was to do a full sweep of the compound and all offices, save for building 4, the call center office. I was not to approach building 4 under any circumstances, no matter what I heard from the outside. Even if I saw someone inside from the windows, I was not to engage. When I asked for more details, they refused to answer me, stating that I should simply obey my orders if I valued my life.

Now, people have a normal 9 to 5 job in that building and nothing seems to be wrong during the day. When I do ask the employees about it during my morning shifts though, they all seem to either not know anything or abruptly find an excuse to end the conversation.

For building 6, the designer company, the rules were even stranger. Here's what the chief told me:

"In building 6, you may sometimes run into someone. A woman, to be precise. She's going to try to start a conversation with you. It is imperative that you ignore her presence at all costs. She will try to talk to you, taunt you, but she will never get in your way. An extremely important rule to remember and I cannot stress this enough, is that if you see her in the building, don't run or exit the building before finishing your sweep. Trust me, she'll know. Do the sweep as you normally would, check every room and then quietly exit, ignoring her all the way. She will become increasingly agitated and violent, might even try to startle you, tell you there's something behind you in a very convincing manner. Just ignore her. If you don't… well, you don't wanna know what happened to the last guard."

I've since encountered the woman once and it was a grueling and agonizing experience I would rather not talk about.

The gate

Another rule I had to remember was not opening the gate between the hours of 22-07. The chief said that under no circumstances am I to open the gate. Even if the next guard comes 5 minutes earlier to relieve me of duty, the gate was to remain closed.

That brings me to the experience I had once. It was about 6 months after I started working and the sun was almost already up. I heard knocking on the gate and when I went out, I saw through the gate the silhouette of my coworker.

"Hey, mind opening the gate?" He asked.

As I approached and put my keys into the keyhole, my phone started ringing. I answered it without even looking at the caller, but when I heard the voice, my blood froze.

It was my coworker.

"Hey, I'm gonna be late 30 minutes today, sorry man!"

I hung up and just then realized it was 6:50 am. I stared at the silhouette on the other side of the gate, who suddenly started banging on the door, demanding to be let in, stating he had lost his cellphone and he was the real coworker. I retreated to the guardhouse and waited for what seemed like forever until the banging stopped. In reality, it only lasted until 7 am. Those were all the rules I had to follow on my own post and most of the time it's uneventful, however I've heard stories from other coworkers.

Dead man walking

Since I'm in contact with guards at other posts, one of them told me this story. He worked as a guard in a residential building and one night an old man who lived there called him to come to his apartment. He didn't explain what was wrong, just told him to go there, so he did. When he reached the apartment, the wife of the old man was crying, stating that her husband was dead. The guard tried convincing her that her man was very much alive and had in fact brought him there, but when he turned around, the old man was gone.

It was then that he saw the old man's dead body in his chair near his sobbing wife. He quit the same night.

Hide and seek

Another creepy thing that happened was on a farmstead which our company has guards posted on. A guy by the name of Jeff who worked there told me about his own experience which made him run away from his post in the middle of the night.

So apparently, the farm was empty at that time since it needed some more stuff built first, but his duty was to basically patrol circles around the farm and make sure there were no squatters or vandals. So one night, as he's walking around he hears someone calling his name in a playful tone. He dismisses it as his imagination at first, but when it recurs, he asks who's there and demands they show up with their hands in the air.

Now I haven't seen this so I can't guarantee anything, but Jeff swears it's true. He says all of a sudden, out of the crops a man just stands up. The top of the crops reach to his waist, which was technically impossible, because the crops themselves were taller than Jeff, and he's a pretty tall guy.

But the man grins at Jeff and continues calling his name playfully, as if he's still hiding from him. Needless to say Jeff didn't stick around to see what the fuck that guy wanted. When he reported it to HQ, they said there were sightings of that man in the past, always calling the names of the guards, but never really doing anything harmful.

Keep the camera off

The next thing I'll share with you here is my experience when I was stationed at a hospital for one month. It was a private clinic of some sorts and my job was to basically monitor the camera feed. Camera 3 was off though, and when I asked why, they told me to keep it that way and never turn it on. They also said that from time to time I may see a person on the feed which covered the outside of the security office and that he would just be standing there, facing the door. I was to remain in my office when that happened and not glance at the door. He would usually disappear after 30 minutes or so. Patrolling was strictly forbidden between the hours of 3am - 6am.

Money is one of the reasons why I haven't quit so far and the dangers aren't that bad once you get used to them and you know what you're doing. And plus getting stationed at different posts keeps the job adventurous and dynamic.

If any of you lack any special talents or qualifications like me, this job is perfect for you.

Ignore the lady

This happened about a year ago, but I still dread going back to the building every time during my patrol. I was doing a sweep of the building, using my flashlight to illuminate my path. As I was done checking one of the offices, as I turned around, my heart nearly popped out of my chest at what the beam of my flashlight landed on. It was a woman in her late twenties, with unkempt hair and raggedy clothes. She was just standing there, staring at me, not even flinching at the light in her face.

I was about to talk to her, thinking she was a squatter, completely forgetting about the rule since I had never once encountered her by then. And then when I remembered the rules, that I was supposed to ignore her, my heart starting to thump fast. I lowered my flashlight to my waist, pretending I was looking at something on the wall to prevent her from seeing my beam bouncing up and down from my trembling hands. I remembered that I had to do a full sweep before leaving if she was here and I was only done with one floor, so at the thought of this I cursed in my mind.

"Hey, I'm sorry, I think I fell asleep in one of the offices and stayed after closing." She said, but I ignored her.

I pretended to look around some more, but knew I could only do it for so long before she got suspicious. So I decided to test my luck and just went for the door. As soon as I was inches close to her, she just stepped aside and let me move along. I strode to the next office, but heard her following me right behind.

"Hey, can you please let me out? My children must be worried sick." She repeated.

The next fifteen minutes or so, she was breathing down my neck, constantly trying to grab my attention. As I entered one of the offices, she pointed to the corner opposite of where my beam was and said:

"Hey, who's that over there?"

I fought the urge to look there, knowing she was lying, but half scared that someone would just jump me right around the corner. As I progressed with my sweep, she became increasingly irritated, throwing stuff in my direction (not at me mind you, but trying to startle me b throwing them in front of my face, etc.), suddenly jumping in my walking path with a loud scream before moving aside again, clasping her hands over her mouth and pointing behind me with wide eyes which screamed utter fear, even saying things like "I know you can see me, I know you know I'm here, I can see how scared you are".

I ignored all her provocations as much as I could and by the time I was back on the first floor, more than ready to get out, she was saying things like "Are you sure you checked all the rooms?", giggling along the way. I put the key in the keyhole and everything went quiet. I didn't wait to see if she was gone, but instead just went out as calmly as I could and locked the door behind me. I couldn't sleep for a few weeks after that.

Hazmat experiment

A few months ago I was stationed at an office building. At first it seemed like a common job, but I knew there was a catch before I even signed up. Sure enough, I was right. My partner and I were stationed on floor 43, which was undergoing renovations. Our job was to simply stand in front of a door. The door had a card reader and we were given access, but were strictly forbidden from entering.

People in hazmat suits would be coming in and out all day long from 8 am - 4 pm. We were to let them in and out as they pleased, keeping track of the number of people who came and went. Now the catch was, after 16:00 we were ordered not to let anyone in or out. That meant even if someone knocked on the door at 16:01 we were to ignore them entirely. There would always be at least three people who'd try to leave the room after 16:00, always asking politely and then becoming increasingly desperate, saying they simply lost track of time and pleading with us, saying that their family was waiting for them home.

We always ignored their crying and pleading, no matter how desperate it was, until it turned into whimpers and then finally stopped. Now I've only seen the room from the door and from what I could see, it was just a normal room undergoing renovations like the rest of the floor, so whatever was in there must have been deeper inside or hidden in plain site. As for the numbers we tracked - the number of people who got out by the end of the day was always lower than the number of people who went in.

Deadly mirror
One story a guard named Chris told me was about his time in an old mansion guarding a big mirror. He and his coworker were in the security room, patrolling every hour, especially making sure that the mirror was covered with the sheet. They were to under no circumstances look at the mirror. They had a camera feed of the mirror which was on the bottom floor under the stairs, but it was turned so that the reflective side faced away from the camera.

This one night, Chris' coworker goes for a patrol and as he enters the mirror room, suddenly the sheet just slides off. Now the guy who told me this said it was technically impossible for the sheet to just come off, because it was fastened tightly, but somehow it did and his partner just finds himself staring at the mirror. Chris locks the security room, as per the instructions from HQ and calls the intervention team. Meanwhile, he glances back at the camera feed, only to find his coworker still staring blankly at the mirror. He thought the camera was frozen, but the timer was moving, so his partner was just very still. He tried radioing him, but there was no response. After about a minute or so, all of a sudden his partner pulls out his gun, puts it in his mouth and blows his brains out.

Chris was transferred the next day since a special team was sent to secure the mirror and his services there were no longer needed.

Singing guard

One position that everyone is massively trying to apply for is the surveillance office in a small town close to my own. Why they want the position is what I'll get to in a bit. So basically, the camera feed on the monitors in HQ over there cover various private households. One of the households is said to have a man in a suit show up at the doorstep from time to time. Now usually, guards need to go out to the address and make sure everything is okay or apprehend the intruder, but for this specific individual, HQ left a very unique guide.

Here are the instructions left by HQ:

If the security official notices an individual in business attire on Camera 12 during his shift, the steps below must be followed when confronting the individual:

1. Approach the individual and wait for him to turn around. He will continue to smile for the entirety of the conversation, but should his expression change, disengage and run to safety as quickly as possible. Be advised that while firearms are not prohibited, they are highly ineffective against the individual. Do not turn or look away from him once he has turned around, unless you need to evacuate.

2. The individual will after turning around inquire "Lovely night, isn't it?". If he has not asked this question, follow the previous step and evacuate.

3. If the individual has inquired the aforementioned

question, respond with "Yes it is. What can I do for you?" or "Indeed it is. How can I help you?". A combination of both works as well. If the individual ceases to smile during this interaction, evacuate immediately.

4. If done correctly, the individual will now ask "Can you sing me a song?". If he says anything else, evacuate.

5. From here, you are to sing the pre-taught song to the individual, while ignoring his taunts and distractions. If so much as one word, pause, tone or stress are missed, evacuate. If the individual stops smiling during the song, evacuate.

6. If done correctly, the individual will say "Splendid! Thank you for the beautiful song!". If he says anything aside from that, evacuate.

7. If step 6 was done correctly, close your eyes for at least 10 seconds and then open them. On the front steps where the individual stood will now be a briefcase, containing a large sum of money, while the individual himself will be gone and the household safe.

8. On the way back, the security official may encounter people of various ages in dire need of help (most common occurrences include starving women with newborn babies, lost children, an attractive young woman hitchhiking, etc.) They are to be ignored and not offered assistance under any circumstances.

9. Return to the post and turn off camera 12

Note: The company does not claim the reward from the individual, therefore the security official is free to keep it.

The high risk- high reward position makes it attractive to many people, but most of them never live to tell the tale. I was also told that the candidates go through rigorous training, focusing primarily on sprinting. The candidates also need to pass the test which simulates the encounter with the businessman no less than 5 times with 95% or higher score. They are forced to remember the song perfectly, going through a computerized scanner which detects any notes which were off. I don't know what the song is, but I was told it's a simple tune which sounds like something taught in preschool.

These things sound attractive due to pay or rush some people thrive on, but a tiny mistake can cost you your life. Or worse.

A walk in the park
Here are some more stories about places that I was
stationed at and the ones I heard from other guards in
the company. A lot of these guards are dead now and
I reckon the same could happen to me at any moment
on my shift, so in case there's a lack of updates, most
likely I met the same fate.

So one memorable experience I have had (and not in
a good way) was when I was stationed at a local park
with another guard. The park wasn't too big – had a
playground, running track which wound in a circle
around the park itself and a tennis court. Everywhere
else around were thick trees, so following the running
track gave a very convincing impression of being in a
forest, away from civilization. My coworker and I
were to start our shift in the park at 7pm and would
end it at 7am. There was a tiny guardhouse near the
entrance which we would spend most of our shift in
and every 2 hours we would go patrolling around the
park, very strictly following the running track where
the path was illuminated. We were given a heavy-
duty flashlight and a backup torch in case the main
one runs out of power. HQ issued an order that if we
found any burnt out light on our path, we were to
retreat to the guardhouse immediately and let
maintenance know about it in the morning. Under no
circumstances were we to step into the dark patch of
the track.

This one night, I was doing my rounds around the
park when all of a sudden, I heard my partner's voice.
He simply shouted "Hey, help me!" from a distance. I
couldn't tell where it was coming from, so I called

out to him, moving my beam across the trees beyond the path. Now, the light we were given is able to penetrate darkness so well that you could see at least 100 feet in front of you. But when I illuminated the area my partner's voice was coming from, there was nothing. Moreover, the voice seemed to change the positions it was coming from.

He yelled again "Hey, help me!". I called out to him once more, but there was no response. I didn't dare wander into the darkness, especially with no signs of him anywhere, heavy-duty light or not. Then my partner yelled for help again and I realized something which made the hairs at the back of my neck stand straight.

His cries for help were on a loop. Always saying the same thing, same intonation, same length of pauses. I even looked at my watch and sure enough, I was right. Call for help, 8 seconds pause. Call for help, 8 seconds pause. I then realized how suddenly quiet everything was. Usually the park was somewhat loud at night – crickets, owls, etc. Now it was so silent I could hear my own heart thumping. I turned around very slowly and walked out of there, doing my best not to sprint as my partner's looping cries for help persisted almost halfway until I was back at the guardhouse.

When I finally got back, my suspicion was confirmed and my partner was there, visibly confused at what I just told him. We called HQ to report suspicious activity and in no less than 5 minutes, a vehicle pulled up at the entrance. An intervention unit emerged, which was essentially an armored and heavily armed team sent in case of emergencies. I was questioned by the team leader for the next hour, while the others went to the scene where I had heard the voice of my coworker.

My partner and I were escorted out of the place and the following morning we were told that the park contract was voided by the company and we no longer needed to go there. I don't know anything else though, because right after that I returned to my original post back at HQ.

Mrs Rogers

I spoke to a former intervention unit member who had worked for the company for over 5 years. He said that some of the shit he had seen was unimaginable and he was willing to share some with me.

For instance, this one time they got a call from a residential building they were securing that there were strange noises coming from one of the rooms. The team arrived on the scene and questioned the guard who reported the incident. Apparently, his job was to make sure no one entered room 416. He explained that the room itself was unoccupied, but that the noises would be heard constantly between 2am and 3am. Usually those noises would include child-like giggling, loud footsteps, bouncing of something on the floor, etc. The residents learned to ignore the noises, but this one old lady, Mrs. Rogers managed to get in, which he saw on the camera feed.

Now the intervention unit was told not to go in after anyone after 20 minutes had passed, but they still had time, so they rushed to the room. The guy who was telling me this said that as they approached the room, they heard voices, like a group of people trying to talk in a hushed tone. He explained that it sounded like kids in school when they're trying to whisper, but were unintentionally loud enough for others to hear.

As soon as they touched the doorknob, the voices stopped in unison. Not like the conversation was over, but literally like someone pressed a mute button in the middle of a sentence. They burst inside the empty room which looked like no one stepped inside for years, weapons raised.

No one was there. And as they were standing there, completely silent, they heard a barely audible, wheezing sound from above. They all looked up and as they did, they froze. The guy who told me this said that what he saw still keeps him up at night sometimes.

Mrs. Rogers was standing on the ceiling like a spider on all fours, craning her head so much they thought her neck was broken and she was looking directly at the unit upside down, wide-eyed. Spit was occasionally dropping from her mouth to the floor, as she was wheezing. Her fingers had somehow mutated into long claws. Then without any warning, Mrs. Rogers had managed to jump down on one of the team members in the blink of an eye and gunshots ensued. He said that by the time they were done shooting, two more members were down and Mrs. Rogers had hundreds of bullet holes in her body and head and was no longer moving.

He encountered similar scenarios after that, but never came so close to dying again. The residents were evacuated from the building indefinitely the next day and the official story given was that there was toxic fungi located within the building.

Extra students

I'll share a story I was told by another guard who went missing later on. He was stationed at a private school and it had a set of very strict rules they had to follow.

First off, there were ten guards in total in each shift and each of them were assigned to a classroom. Their job was to count all the students after the classes were over. Should any of the students go missing, they were to call HQ immediately.

Now comes the weird part. One day, the guard who told me this story counted all the kids in class and the final number didn't add up. Instead of 32 students, he has 33. He counted a few times to make sure and when the number was confirmed as 33, he told the teacher to start calling on them by name and separating them from the group one by one. The teacher did so, calling each and every student, but when they were done, there are no surpluses. The list showed 32 and 32 were called on and yet 33 students were in the classroom. They couldn't tell who the extra student was even when the guard was watching them like a hawk to make sure none of them would sneak to the group of called on kids while they weren't looking. Baffled and unsure what to do, the guy told the teacher to keep an eye on them while he contacts HQ. Already feeling silly for contacting the higher-ups over an extra student rather than a missing one, he expected HQ to scold him for calling about something like that.

But when he said that he had an extra student who

just popped up, chuckling at the absurdity of the situation, the person on the other end of the line suddenly went silent. She asked him to repeat what he said and when he did, the woman told him to get the teacher out of there, lock the classroom immediately and radio everyone else to do the same at once. He did so and only minutes later the intervention unit arrived, escorting the guards out of there. He said he has no idea what happened next, but when he returned to the school the next day for his shift, everything seemed to be normal.

No one really knows what the company is dealing with here. Not even intervention was told what these encounters are, since it seems to be a very strict need-to-know basis. One thing's for sure though.

When I hear some of these stories from other guards, I realize how lucky I got to run into some of these creatures and live to tell the tale.

Missing partner

I want to start off by clarifying one thing. The company I work for is *not* the SCP. I know there are a lot of similarities between the encounters which I described and some of the SCP files, but my company has nothing to do with that. We are just as I stated before, a standalone security company that provides technical security, surveillance and physical protection services to clients.

While I was stationed at an office complex similar to the one in HQ where I am now, I had a number of strange experiences. Our job was mostly staying in the guardhouse and conducting mandatory patrols around the complex at the start and at the end of the shift, one guard taking one side while I took the other.

A few months back, I came to my shift as usual with my partner. So on that day we finished our initial patrol and returned to the guardhouse. We usually talk to pass the time, but this time he seemed unapproachable and quiet, so I figured I should leave him alone and continued to read my book for the time being.

Our shift was almost over when we decided to do our final sweep, so we split up to do our rounds. After I was done, I came back, but my partner wasn't there. I figured he wasn't done with his sweep yet, so I shrugged it off and continued passing the time. When he wasn't back in over 30 minutes though, I radioed him. No response. He was nowhere on the cameras, either. Figuring he may be in trouble, I went out to search for him, frustrated that he wasn't back and it was almost the end of our shift. As I was patrolling, I saw him in the distance across the parking lot, turned away from me and looking at something. I called out his name and he turned around. I waved to him, telling him to get back and he waved back to me. I took it as a signal that he understood what I said and returned to the guardhouse. The guys from the next shift were already there and I went home, telling them my partner would do the debriefing. Not two hours later, I got a phone call from the same guys.

They told me my partner never showed up, so they went looking for him, thinking something may have been wrong. Sure enough, soon after they started the search, he was found dead. I was shocked, to say the least. I asked them when he had died and how, since I had seen him literally minutes before they arrived. They told me that it wasn't possible for me to see him then. I asked why and the answer they gave me chilled me to the bone.

Apparently he died about 10 hours ago. The camera recordings confirmed it. He was seen wandering off camera into the garage and then never seen coming out. One of the guys discovered his body there, no visible wounds or marks on him. HQ recovered his body, but shared no details about the cause of his death.

So that begs the question. If he died 10 hours ago, who the fuck did I see in that parking lot? And moreover, who in fuck's name was with me in the guardhouse for 10 hours between patrols?

Looping stairs
In that same place, in addition to our patrol around
the complex we also had to check inside buildings
and make sure everything was alright. So one time on
my shift I was in one of the office buildings doing my
sweep on the second floor and I moved to the stairs to
get to the next floor. I climbed up and as I did, I saw
that the sign on the wall said 'second floor' again. I
dismissed it, thinking I must have been on the first
floor prior to this and just got confused. I moved up
one floor and again, the sign said 'second floor'. I
stared at the sign in bafflement and decided to try the
door. Locked. I climbed up one more floor and again,
I was on the second floor. I knew by this point
something was wrong. I mean the building itself has
only three floors and I had already climbed at least
four.

I decided to descend the stairs as fast as I could, but
every time I passed by the floor sign, it said second
floor. I ran until I was exhausted, trying doors along
the way, all of which were locked. I leaned over the
railing to look down the stairs and saw the staircase
going down infinitely into a black abyss, same for
above. I radioed my partner, but there was no
response. No signal on the phone, either. I decided to
sit down and think about everything, already half-
accepting my impending demise.

It must have been hours there that I sat and ran down
the stairs intermittently when I suddenly heard the
sound of door opening below. I was so relieved to
actually hear something besides my own footsteps
that I didn't even think about the potential dangers it

might entail. I rushed down and to my relief, saw the sign for floor one, the door open as I had left it when I entered the building. I bolted out of there and straight to the guardhouse, barging in through the door.

My coworker was reading the newspaper, only shooting me a glance before returning to his reading. When I accused him for not answering his radio, he looked confused, stating he never got any call from me. I asked him why he hadn't looked for me when I hadn't returned in hours and again, he looked confused. He glanced at his watch and then at me and simply said:

"You've been gone for five minutes."

HQ issued a rule after that. The office building was off limits for all personnel after 8 pm.

Copy partner
One time during my shift, as I was finishing my patrol, I heard my coworker's voice in the distance. He sounded like he was in distress, so I followed the sound, calling out his name. As I approached the source of the voice, it became obvious that my coworker was in the looping building, begging me to help him. I drew my gun and told him to hold on, ready to risk my life for my partner and just as I was about to enter… I heard his voice behind me, calling my name.

I turned around and sure enough, there he was. I looked back at the building and the cries from the person in the building stopped completely. The coworker confirmed it wasn't him who was in the building and as I turned back to the source of the voice, I could only mutter to myself "you sneaky son of a bitch".

Impostor in the guardhouse

One thing that happened to one of the other guys during one of the shifts still puts me on edge. The guy named Chris was in the guardhouse with his partner and the partner decided to go for a patrol earlier. Chris continued reading his book as the partner left the place. One minute later he heard the door shut behind him and the thud of his footsteps of his partner inside.

"Forget something, huh?" He asked, not looking up from his book.

The partner put his hand on Chris' shoulder and Chris raised his head, ready to turn around.

And as he raised his head, he saw his coworker pass next to the window outside. Chris froze, staring at the window, at the reflection of the figure standing behind him. He said he felt the grip on his shoulder tightening. Bracing himself as well as he could, he swiftly turned around drawing his gun and pointing it at… nothing.

No one was there. I checked the recordings of the camera feed in the guardhouse and sure enough, no one was there with him. I could see Chris on the camera sitting up, visibly becoming tense and turning around with his gun drawn before looking around and finally holstering the weapon. He looked like a crazy person from this angle.

I never figured what that was, or the other occurrences in the complex, but HQ issued new orders shortly after. The guards who were on the shift were to stay together at all times, even patrolling in pairs and communicating via code sentences every 30 minutes to ensure their partner wasn't an impostor.

Invisible people

Chris told me of another incident he had during one of his shifts. He said that he saw someone suspicious on camera in front of one of the offices way after working hours, so he went to investigate. Halfway through, the partner radioed him and said he lost the person out of sight. It was strange though, because apparently he only turned around for one second and the guy on the camera was gone. However he said he thought he noticed movement on the camera which overlooked the windows of the office from the outside. He said it was on the second floor.

Chris decided to investigate it. As he was doing his sweep on the second floor, his partner radioed him again halfway into his patrol and asked him if he found anyone. Chris said no, asking him if he saw anything on camera. The partner first sayid no and then he paused mid-sentence. Chris asked him to confirm what he said and the partner told him he should come back to the guardhouse. Chris wanted to finish the sweep, but the partner insisted he come back to the guardhouse at once. Frustrated, he returned and asked what was wrong.

"You really didn't see anyone in there?" The partner asked.

When Chris said no, the partner called him over to look at one of the camera feeds. He rewound the footage to where he could see Chris in the window with the flashlight and told him to pay close attention. Chris wasn't alone there.

When his beam flashed across the window, it caught a silhouette staring at the camera. The next few seconds of the recording were spent by him talking to his partner on the radio and in addition to the window silhouette there was now a person standing directly behind him. As Chris moved through the room, more and more people came into view, all staring directly at him, while he was completely oblivious to their presence. After that he saw himself exiting the building, while the people in the building were disappearing, or more like, blending in with the darkness.

Overall, I've worked in various fucked up places, but this one seems to be the most dangerous and aggressive one, with even HQ not being able to predict some of the outcomes. If any of you know of anyone who has similar experiences to mine as a security guard, chances are we work for the same company.

Don't close the doors
The story I'm going to tell you is about a big office building our company has a contract with. I never personally worked there, but some of the guys I know did. One of the guards told me about the place in more detail. Apparently, it's a normal office building where people work a regular 9-5 job, but our guards need to be there 24-7. From around 8 am until 6 pm until all employees leave, it's pretty leisure. However the guards and the employees have one very strict rule to follow.

The building has no doors, including the one at the entrance. So at first glance, it looks really strange to see all these offices, bathrooms, etc, with naked door frames. After the employees leave, guards are to conduct patrols every hour until the end of the shift. They have to make sure all the door frames have no doors on them and should they spot an actual door anywhere on the premise, they are to make sure it isn't closed.

If the door was open or at least left slightly ajar, the guards would need to put one of those door holders on the ground, to prevent the door from closing. The guards would carry a bunch of door holders on patrols just for this purpose. If the door was closed however, they were ordered not to go near it under any circumstances.

They also had a map of the building and had to memorize where each room was, making sure that the layout of the rooms was exactly how it was on the map, including the direction the office desks and furniture were facing, etc.

Now, the guard who told me this shared his own experience with me. He said that everything was calm for the first few months and then during one of his night shift patrols, he ran into a door on the second floor which was slightly ajar. He could see an office space behind the door and following the instructions, he pulled out his door holder and went to put it in front of the door.

However as he did so, he apparently stumbled forward and actually pushed the door, which shut with a loud click. He swears he couldn't have just fallen like that, so he firmly believes something or someone somehow made him fall. When he saw that he accidentally shut the door, the guy panicked and decided to push everything under the rug by quickly opening the door, hoping no one would notice. But he says that when he opened it, the office was no longer there. He was instead looking at the bathroom.

He thought he was in the wrong place at first, because there was no way the bathroom would be there. So when he double checked the map, sure enough, he was right. The office space he initially saw was supposed to be there. So he closed the door and opened it again. This time he was staring at the kitchen. Fascinated by the whole thing, he kept closing and opening the door over and over, seeing all the different rooms from the building.

He said he would have gone on some more, but his partner radioed him to ask him how far in he was with his sweep. The guy ended up closing and opening the door for a few more minutes until he finally saw that same office again. He placed the door holder on the floor and bolted back to the security room. He reported the appearance of the door to HQ, leaving out the details about closing and opening it.

Everything was fine that night, but the following morning he was called by his boss, who asked him what the fuck he was thinking closing the door like that. The guard was confused about how his boss knew about it. The boss told him that apparently, some of the rooms had shifted around and now the entire office building was completely jumbled up.

No one was harmed and nothing really happened other than that, save for the only inconvenience being the workers having to make their way from the third floor all the way to the ground floor to use the bathrooms. He continued working, but never saw another door there again.

House of rules

One specific story which stands out for me is from a guard who was stationed as security in a residential house between 9 pm and 4 am. The owners, a married couple lived there and they would leave the house every night at 8 pm and the guard who was appointed, was told by the owners that the duties are fairly simple. HQ briefed the guard before he started working by giving him a list of rules to follow. Here's the transcript of the written rules:

Duty starts at 9 pm, however make sure to be there at least 1 hour earlier. Before leaving your home for duty, take a sharp object and leave it inside your home near the exit (for instance on the shoe stand). Any sharp object will do, however the sharper the better (preferably something that can easily puncture the skin). If you can't make it at least 30 min before 9 pm to the house where you perform your duty, inform HQ and skip your shift.

Do not attempt to enter the house at or after 9 pm under any circumstances. Once inside and the owners leave, follow these rules carefully:

9 pm – 10 pm: You can move freely throughout the house, with the exception of entering the basement.

10 pm – 11 pm: Stay in the living room during the entire hour. Do not leave the room under any circumstances. Do not leave the house, either. If you need to use the bathroom, use a bottle or any other means.

11 pm – 11:23 pm: You will hear someone knocking on the window. Avoid looking at it. The knocking may become relentless and loud, but do not look at it. You may turn on the TV for distraction.

11:23 pm – 00 am: The knocking will have stopped by now, but you now may hear children crying upstairs. Ignore it. No children reside in the house.

00 am - 00:25 am: You may move freely around the first floor of the house, although it is advised you stay in the living room / kitchen area and prepare for the next step.

00:25 am – 00:30 am: Below the sink in the kitchen is a bucket full of fresh meat. Take it to the basement. You do not need to enter the basement, you can simply leave the bucket near the door inside, but make sure to close and lock the door again. A very important thing to note here: make sure you do not spill or drop any blood or meat from the bucket on the floor anywhere outside the basement, since it can accurately smell blood up to a mile away. If you happen to spill any blood, do not bother cleaning. Simply follow the next step.

00:30 am – 1 am: You may hear growling noises coming from the basement, but do not bother investigating. If you have previously spilled any blood around the house, sit on the couch. Turn on the TV and turn up the volume to the max. Clasp your ears with your hands and keep your eyes firmly shut. Face the ground and stay in this position until 1 am. If there is a pause on the TV for more than a few

*seconds, try to produce any loud sound of your own
by screaming or speaking loudly to drown out any
unnatural noises you may hear.*

*1 am – 2 am: You may freely move throughout the
entire house again (basement excluded). This is the
time to use for bathroom breaks. Do not attempt to
leave the house. You should also use this time to
memorize the room layouts (furniture, specifically).
During this hour, you may hear a voice coming from
the bedroom on the second floor. If you do,
investigate. If there is a man in the room, lock the
door and return to the living room immediately. Do
not attempt to talk to the man. If the room is empty,
you may continue to move freely.*

*2 am – 3:33 am: Nothing major will happen during
this hour. Ignore any ringing of the phone. Do not
pick it up no matter how much it rings*

*3:33 am – 3:55 am : Now is the time to take stock of
all the furniture in the house. If you see any extra
furnishing, do not sit on it or touch it in any way. You
will start to feel extremely sleepy by this point.
Whatever you do, you must not fall asleep. It is
recommended you spend this time in the kitchen and
leave the sink water running, so you can splash your
face whenever your eyelids become too heavy.*

*3:55 am – 4 am: The owners will have returned by
now. Before leaving, make sure to say aloud the
sentence "My duty is finished.". Not that if you do not
do it, upon entering to your home, you will find that
you are back in the house of the owners. Should this*

be the case, then you only have one option – take the sharp object you left close to the door and inflict mild damage to yourself (minor stab in the forearm or hand, etc). If the house doesn't change to your own home, repeat the previous step until it does.

He quit after just one night.

No one leaves
There was a place I was supposed to work in, but luckily said no. This was apparently a big lodge deep inside a forest and HQ had a ton of people waiting in line to work there. There were no duties there. No guarding, no paranormal rules, nothing.

So when I asked what's the catch, they said the guards can never leave the place until another one takes over. When I laughed, the chief stared at me. He went on to explain that there have been cases of people wanting to quit in the middle of their shifts, but whenever they try to, something happens which prevents them from leaving. Either a huge storm, an accident, injury, suddenly coming down with a fever severe enough to stop them from moving, etc. One guy even tried calling his friend to pick him up, but the friend ended up getting lost in the woods. Another guy tried leaving despite the thick snowstorm, but as he trekked through the snow, he ended up right back at the house. He claims there was no way he could have been back there since he only went straight, and yet there he was.

HQ has all these guards in line ready to take over, in case someone fails to show up for their shift own and the guard who was previously there is stranded. They still don't know how the lodge works or why anyone has to be there, but all they do know is that one person always has to be there. The even stranger thing – no one in HQ knows how and when they signed a contract for this place. Whoever the client is, he sends payments to the company every month and is impossible to track down.

The hole
One of the guards told me that he worked in a residential building. The building itself was normal, but in the basement of the building was a big, round hole. No one knew how it got there and the residents said they just woke up to find it there one day. The old lady who discovered it almost fell inside when she went to retrieve her bicycle.

Various survey and research teams were sent to investigate the hole, but oddly enough, no equipment could determine where the bottom was. Electronics would stop working at a certain depth, throwing something inside produced no sound of impact, chemical lights got swallowed by the darkness, etc. They sent one crew member down there, but after about 10 minutes of descending, he stopped responding. They pulled him out as fast as they could, but he was gone. All that was left of him was the pile of clothes he was wearing, still attached to the safety gear and ropes.

The company was appointed to stand guard in front of the basement and not let anyone in. The guard who worked there, Andy, told me the job was pretty leisure most nights, except that he was bored. Then one night, he heard something coming from inside the basement. It sounded like someone calling his name. At first he thought it was his imagination, but the more he listened, the more he became convinced it was his sister.

Despite getting instructions from HQ not to go near

the hole, mostly due to the possibility of slipping and falling, Andy opened the door. Sure enough, there it was. His sister's voice, calling him, right from the hole, clear as a day. He asked her how she got there and if she was okay and she perkily said that everything was fine. She asked Andy to come down there so they could talk. She talked in such a nonchalant way that Andy became suspicious of the whole situation.

She asked him again to come down. Andy refused, telling her that he would call help, to which his sister became increasingly agitated and angry. She demanded that he come down there and help her. Andy didn't budge and his sister said that he would let her die there, just like he let their father die. Andy froze to this and his sister uttered a single sentence which made Andy run out of there.

"Andy, life is nothing but a pile of shit." Those were his father's last words before he killed himself in front of Andy.

Andy bolted out of the building, listening to his sister calling after him and begging him to come down. Andy called HQ, telling them he was never going back. He was assigned to a different post and never had a problem again. The really weird thing about this whole experience was that no one but Andy knew what his father's last words were. He never told anyone that he watched him turn the gun on himself and just stuck to the story that he found him dead.

But the weirdest of all things was the fact that his

sister had died in a tragic car accident four years before he ever saw the hole. The basement was locked tightly afterwards and guards continued working there, but they all reported the same thing. Voices of their loved ones calling from the hole and always asking the one, same thing – to come down.

The Giggler
The intervention guy whose story I shared in one of the earlier updates told me another one recently, which chilled me to the bone. He and his unit were stationed at a long-since abandoned hotel. They'd get to do whatever they wanted in the hotel, but at exactly 4:25 am they had to assemble at the reception desk.

Their job was to sweep the entire area for any suspicious activity. The guy who told me this said HQ never told them who or what they were looking for, but they were ordered to shoot on sight upon seeing anyone besides the unit members in the hotel.

They had been sweeping the hotel four nights in a row at exactly 4:30 am until 5 am, but never found traces of anyone. And then on the fifth night, as they checked the second floor, the commander of the unit ordered them to stop and be quiet. There was a sound of muffled giggling coming from somewhere on the floor. Strangely though, as they listened, the giggling was always the same intonation and length of pause. Giggle. Five seconds pause. Giggle. Five seconds pause. He described it as an adult trying to impersonate a child's giggle.

Carefully, the unit followed the sound to one of the rooms and as they stood in front of the door, the giggling became louder and more frequent. The unit burst inside the room and pointed their guns at the source of the sound.

Facing the window was a tall person. Except it wasn't a person. Here's how the guy who told me this described the creature. A very round face, which contrasted its impossibly thin body. It had extremely long arms and legs and it was so inhumanely tall that it had to hunch over and bend its knees in order to avoid touching the ceiling. It giggled again, and it still sounded muffled, just as it did behind a closed door.

The unit stood there, with their guns pointed at this thing, as the creature giggled once more, before going silent. And then it slowly started to turn around and locked eyes with the unit. The creature apparently had a grinning, toothy, round face with large, unblinking eyes and this took the unit aback so much that they froze.

It giggled again, but this time it was deeper and more guttural, albeit still muffled. Just then the creature started running towards the unit, all the while giggling, louder and faster than ever. Everyone fired at will, practically emptying their clips into the thing. Luckily, the Giggler, as he was later dubbed by the intervention unit, never managed to reach them and fell backwards as soon as the force of the bullets connected with it. As it lay there on the ground, it apparently kept giggling some more, but the sound became slower and more quiet, until it completely stopped, leaving the creature dead, with its grinning face never changing.

The commander informed HQ about this, who told them that their mission was complete and they no longer needed to stay in the hotel. The intervention guy concluded that two of the unit members committed suicide within two months after the mission. In their farewell notes, they said they could no longer stand to listen to the giggling at night.

The man with the sideways face

Recently, I was transferred to the operators' room in HQ. Essentially, I'd sit in a room with a lady who served as backup for various guards who found themselves in situations they couldn't resolve. Most of the situations were your run-of-the-mill cases, where guards had drunks trespassing or being unsure if they should investigate certain sounds, etc.

There was only one call that I witnessed which stood out for me. It was late night and we got a call from a guard who was stationed on a private farm. Whenever a call came through, I'd put on the extra pair of earphones which would allow me to hear the conversation. Here's the transcript of the conversation.

Operator: This is HQ, what's your situation?

Guard: Uh, yeah. This is Mark from the Spencer farm. There's a guy standing in front of the barn. I can see him on the camera.

O: ...Alright?...

G: He's been standing there for two hours now. I first thought the camera was frozen, but when I zoomed in just now, I can see his fingers are moving. He's tapping them nervously on his thigh. And, wait... his head seems to be twitching slightly.

O: Is he armed?

G: I can't see from here, he's facing away from the

camera, but I don't see anything in his hands.

O: He's standing on private property, you need to warn him to leave right away.

G: Yeah. Yeah, I'll do that right away.

O: Stay on the call while you do so and tell me if you need backup.

Five minutes later, we heard the guard's voice over the call again.

G: Sir? Sir! Sir, can you hear me?

There was a moment of silence.

O: What's going on over there?

G: He isn't responding. He's just standing and twitching there. His twitching is getting more and more violent. I think something's wrong with him.

O: Get him off the property.

G: Sir? I'm going to have to ask you to-

There was a loud scream that came from the guard. The operator pressed him to respond what was wrong, but the guard kept screaming and panting on the line, followed by the sound of frantic footsteps. There was a sound of door violently shutting and shuffling, before the guard quieted down and tried to calm his breathing as much as he could.

O: Mark, I need you to talk to me. What's going on?

The guard' voice came through in a whisper.

G: Can't talk. He's right outside.

By this point I had already called the intervention unit, who said they would arrive on the scene in 10 or so minutes.

O: Mark, can you get somewhere safe? Backup will be there in 10 minutes, but I need you to hide. Can you do that?

G: I-I'm inside the locker. He's standing just outside the security room. Something's wrong with his face.

O: What do you mean?

G: It's all wrong. It's like, it's sideways. His head is normal and all, but the eyes, nose and mouth are all flipped sideways. I think... I think he's calling my name... Oh god, he's coming inside.

There was a sound of door creaking open and then a set of slow and deliberate footsteps. Mark's breathing became stifled as he tried to steady it, probably clasping a hand over his mouth. And then another voice came through, a raspy voice, which sounded as if the person on the other end had something stuck in their throat and difficulty speaking:

"M-MAA-AR-K" It said.

Mark's breathing suddenly became more violent and then he started screaming and begging for his life. The call ended and the operator and I stared at each other in disbelief.

The intervention team arrived on the scene soon. There was no trace of Mark or the man that attacked him. The camera feed showed Mark approaching the man, who then turned around to face the guard, and then Mark running back to the security room. From there the man followed Mark to the security room, taking slow, unsteady steps, twitching along the way. He opened the locker where Mark hid himself. Then the camera feed cut out.

On the frames where the man was facing the camera, I could see his face clearly. It was exactly as Mark had described it – as if the man's face was rotated to the left by 90 degrees. A pair of eyes staring blankly sideways on top of one another and a mouth which looked like a smile, but was instead just a crooked slit. Mark was never seen again.

Secret experiment

My next story is going to be from another intervention unit member. He was stationed at some experimental facility and didn't wanna share any details about its location or nature of the experiment, because as he said, more than his job would be at stake. He spent about five months there with his unit and never saw any action. The regular security guards like me, who were stationed there, were taking care of the mundane problems like trespassers, etc.

However his unit regularly had drills in case of any emergency scenarios. He said the drills were not the typical military kind, but that there were some rules they needed to know, which pertained to not getting into any kind of physical contact with civilians. Their main objective in the worst-case scenario was to seal off all exit points.

Sure enough, one day an alarm sounded in the facility and he and his team got ready to start their mission. As they made their way through the facility, they ran into various dead scientists and other staff members. And then they ran into a survivor. A researcher, all bloody and scared. He raised his hands and begged them not to shoot, while the unit just kept barking orders at him to keep his distance. The researcher kept saying that he's 'not infected', whatever that meant. And as he stood there, eyeing everyone, all of a sudden he snarled, showing rows of sharp teeth which were not there a second ago. And then he lunged forward, tackling one unit member and sinking his teeth into his face.

The guy told me they started shooting long before he even lunged, but it was as if the researcher didn't even react to the bullets. He was riddled with holes and bled, but just kept biting and biting, until he finally just fell over. He tried to jump again, but died a second later. The unit members emptied their clips into the now dead scientist and proceeded to leave the facility, leaving their one dead team member behind.

Once they secured the facility and locked every exit point, locking the potential survivors inside, they contacted HQ and a bunch of armored vehicles with military personnel and hazmat suits showed up. The unit was dismissed from the facility and warned not to talk about any sensitive details related to the experiment, names of staff members, etc. No matter how much I pressed him, he refused to tell me more.

Hive mind

The story which I'm going to share here is from a guard named Tom, who worked in an office building. Before he got sent to work, HQ gave him a one-week training. He was strictly forbidden from talking or making any kind of vocal sounds while working in the office. Communication with his partner by talking was forbidden too, so they used hand signals.

Upon arriving on his first day, Tom saw people doing their everyday jobs at their desks, typing away, but never talking to each other or anyone else. They wouldn't even look at him, but would instead stare at their screens all day. Tom followed HQ's instructions and conducted his duties, not talking to anyone. Then one day he brought his cell to work because he was bored.

As he made his way through the office, someone started calling him and the song which was set as his caller tone blared in the office. He quickly turned it off, but then realized something terrible. All eyes in the office were fixed on him. The people had stopped typing and working and just stared at Tom with an expressionless face. Tom mumbled 'shit' to himself and everyone in the office unanimously said 'SHIT' in a synchronized tone.

Tom slowly made his way out and as he went through the hall, he saw through the glass the people were still staring at him. Not only them though, but everyone else in the office stared at Tom as well. He locked himself in the security room along with the partner and eventually the people returned to their normal, talkless work.

The next day Tom was fired for bringing his phone to work and potentially putting himself and his partner in danger. He said it's a good thing too, because he planned on quitting anyway.

Radio tower

One of the guys from my company named Gary, was outsourced to a small secretive organization for a short project. The details of the project were undisclosed, but the guard who volunteered for this job had to stay in a remote facility with a radio tower, close to a small town for one month.

Now, the organization was pretty shady, since they had military personnel guarding the facility and scientists running around, which raised the question of whether a guard was even needed there. Immediately upon arrival, the superiors explained his duties to him. The guard was free to do anything he wanted all day, but once a day at lunch time, he would need to distribute mint candy to everyone in the facility and make sure they ate it – everyone including himself. He was to make sure the mint was ingested by inspecting each individual's mouth upon swallowing. Anyone who refused was to be reported to the superiors.

Gary laughed at this initially, but when the superiors assured him that this task is of utmost importance, he knew better than to screw around. Gary followed the rules and made sure to have everyone eat mint every day, which caused him to be shunned by a lot of the project participants, since no one knew why they had to do it.

Towards the end of the project however, some people started complaining about frequent headaches – those same people were later exposed as ones who didn't ingest the mint properly. They were detained for insubordination. Something else happened in the meantime however, and the company lost contact with the facility. Of all the people, Gary managed to contact the company with a simple text message that said 'Something wrong, send help now'. An intervention unit was dispatched right away, but it would be three days until they reached the remote area. Before they did however, HQ continued trying to contact Gary and the facility, asking what happened. After days of radio silence they only got one, short text.

Everything okay.

When the intervention unit arrived, everyone at the facility was dead. Details were undisclosed.

Truck driver

There was a security guard in our company who primarily worked as a driver. His job was to transport company-related equipment like weapons, cameras, uniforms, etc. from one facility to another. This sounds like a normal day-to-day job, right? Wrong. As the driver, he took a route which went via an old road and saved a lot of time, but he had a bunch of rules he had to follow. Before he was hired, he had a simulation of the drive, in order to see if he can follow all rules. Here are the rules as listed by HQ below:

Start driving at exactly 9 pm when the alarm in the vehicle goes off, not a minute sooner, not a minute later. Keep all doors locked at all times and keep your seatbelt off for a quicker exit in case of an emergency.
The road is straightforward and there are no turns, so if you see a forking in the road, turn your vehicle around immediately and go back to HQ.

Do not stop for any hitchhikers under any circumstances, even if they are in fatal trouble.

If you see headlights suddenly appearing behind you, speed up.

Ignore any sounds from the back of the vehicle (you may hear banging, growling or clattering).

Don't stare at the rearview mirror for longer than three seconds at a time.

If you see something running along with your vehicle on the side of the road, ignore it no matter how close it is and speed up. It should disappear within five minutes.

If your vehicle's engine suddenly dies, close your eyes, try to stay calm and start the engine again. Ignore any tapping on the windows and do not look at them.

Once you go over the yellow line on the road, which is 24 miles from the starting point, you're in the clear.

Despite seeing all of this in the past few years of his work, he says he wouldn't trade his job for anything in the world.

Morgue

A guy named Ethan told me about his experience working in a morgue. Now, working in a morgue is bad enough as it is, but working in a morgue outsourced to my company is hell. His job was to take over once the staff were done there at 10 pm and just make sure no one got in… or out.

He quit after only a month, due to the mental stress he experienced during his time there. He says the company allowed him to do whatever he wanted there, including sleep, however it wasn't advised and you'll understand why in a moment.

Ethan said that on a good night, he'd hear people screaming from the body chambers, begging to be let out and that they were placed there by mistake. While there was no strict rule about opening the chambers, it would probably be nerve-wracking to do so. The problem however was, that once the bodies started screaming, the only way to stop them was to pull out the chamber. Immediately upon coming into view, Ethan would be faced with a cold, dead, unmoving body and silence would return to the room.

He said that often, when reading something or getting sleepy, he'd feel a strong grip on his shoulder or hear a loud 'boo!' in his ear. There would never be anything around though, but you can see why sleeping there would be impossible.

He'd often see a body chamber pulled out on his way back from the bathroom and if that was the case, his job was to push it back in immediately. There were some other rules, but all in all, what made him quit was a man in a lab coat he constantly kept seeing in the morgue. The company told him never to address the man, since no morgue workers were there after 10 pm.

Ethan made the mistake of talking to him on his first shift and then every subsequent night, the man would silently follow him, always at the same distance and never talking. Just staring at him.

It's all in your head
Another guard who worked in a factory complex with a partner told me a story. He said that he'd been working there for about two months before things got weird. At the start of each shift, he'd meet up with his partner and they'd take turns patrolling. The first month, his partner kept complaining of severe insomnia and fatigue and then one day just came to work completely fresh. The guy who told me the story said he jokingly told his partner he may have been looking at another person with such a sudden change.

That working area was pretty desolate and HQ would rarely contact them – they'd just have them submit reports weekly and that's it. But two months after this guy started working there, HQ contacted the guy and told him to bear working alone for just a few more nights, since there's a new guard on the way. The guy asked 'what do you mean, just a few more nights? I already have a partner here'. HQ went silent for a moment before saying that his partner was found dead at his home a month ago.

As soon as they told him that, as if on cue, he stopped seeing his partner altogether. He said that he saw a change of at least five more guards in the following year.

Don't open the door
One veteran guard told me about the time he spent
guarding a mansion. The mansion itself supposedly
belonged to a late rich man and his family was trying
to sell the place, but apparently no one wanted it,
even though it was dirt-cheap. The guy who told me
the story had been there for almost a year before he
got a new partner, a rookie who had just joined the
company. Apparently there were no rules or anything
like that, except one – don't open any doors.

Well long story short, the rookie messed up. During
his patrol on the second floor, he heard a little girl
crying. Now I don't know if he stopped to think
rationally for a moment or his hero instincts just
kicked in, but he decided to check it out – just a quick
peek. The sobbing was coming from one of the rooms
on the left, so carefully and quietly, he turned the
knob and opened the door. As soon as he did, the
crying stopped. Not like someone had heard him and
then stopped crying, no. This was like someone had
pressed the mute button in the middle.

Anyway, he poked his head in and saw nothing, so he
went back to his patrol. Not a minute later, he heard
the crying again, once more from the left, but
different room. He checked it out again and once
more, the crying stopped. He continued his patrol and
just then realized – the corridor was on a loop.

He continued walking through, hoping it's just a
really long corridor, but every dozen steps or so that
he took, the crying followed him in one of the rooms
on the left. He tried running back, but again, there

was crying on the left and the corridor went on for much longer than he remembered walking. He continued, fully aware that he should have been out by now, but the exit was nowhere in sight.

He was now in full-blown panic, so he contacted his partner via radio, telling him he fucked up. When the veteran asked him how and the rookie told him the corridor was on a loop, the only thing the veteran guard was able to mutter was 'oh fuck'. A moment of silence ensued, before the veteran said:

"You opened the door, didn't you? I told you not to open any fucking doors, what the hell were you thinking?! Alright, listen. Just walk forward. Don't run, just walk. And don't turn around at any sounds behind you, just keep walking, got it? Just pretend you're on your patrol and ignore anything you see or hear. But if you see the crying girl in front of you, you turn around and run for your life, you got it?"

The next few minutes were a mixture of deadly silence and eager anticipation. Ten minutes later though, the rookie stumbles into the security room, pale as a sheet of paper, but alive. He was unable to speak properly due to the trauma, but was uninjured. The veteran called the medical team and they escorted the rookie out of there. He never came back to that place again. Whether he was fired or decided to quit, we never found out.

Black-eyed people
Back when I worked in one of the office buildings that our company guards, I had a partner on duty who would help me in my patrols, since the building was too big. Usually we'd divide patrols with one of us starting from the top floor and moving down and the other guard going from the bottom up until we met on floor 10. To make things interesting, we made a race out of it.

So this one time I started from the bottom and made my way up and met my partner on the 9th floor. At first, I found it odd that he was on this floor, when we always met on floor 10. He said he got tired of waiting upstairs and decided to make his way down and do my work for me. I found it odd that he got there so quickly, since he usually takes his time checking every nook and cranny, but I eventually dismissed it as unimportant. There was something else off here though, but I couldn't put my finger on it. All I know is that I suddenly got a really bad feeling and the hairs on the back of my neck stood straight. Again, I dismissed it as my imagination.

He suggested we return downstairs and head outside so he can have a quick smoke. I reminded him that we were forbidden from doing so, but he said he'd be quick, 2 minutes tops. I was adamant about not going with him, but before we could discuss it further, I heard a voice shout from upstairs:

"Hell yeah, beat you to it! Running late tonight, are we?"

It was my partner's voice. I stared at my partner in

front of me, who looked equally scared and begged me not to go there and told me that the voice was fake. It was then that I realized what was so wrong with the person in front of me. He had completely black eyes. I remember thinking how the fuck didn't I notice that before and bolted upstairs to floor 10. My partner was there, visibly confused by my state. I explained what happened and when we went downstairs, the impostor was gone.

We spoke to HQ about it a bit later and here's what the chief said:

"Ever heard of those black eyed kids?"

My partner and I shook our heads. The chief continued:

"Well apparently there are these kids with black eyes that knock on your door and ask you to let them in. You're not in any danger, so long as you decline their invitation. Now there have been sightings in that building of black eyed adults. They usually ask you to go outside with them, so our assumption is they wanna get out, but can't do it without permission or escort. That's why you're not allowed outside during your shift."

"So what if we let them out?" I asked.

"Don't." Is all the chief said.

Man-eating plants

Another place my company has a contract with is a big botanical garden. Four guards work there in shifts and the rules are simple – carry a flamethrower with you and kill anything find on trails. That includes squatters, stray animals, etc, but the biggest concern were the plants. The guards were told that if they so much as hear something or see a stray root or branch on the trail, unleash hell until everything is sterile again.

Each section of plants was separated in a way that flames couldn't spread to the adjacent ones. This story was shared to me by one of the former guards who retired recently. He said he spent about ten years working there and had seen all sorts of things, but most commonly he'd just have to burn the plants that have grown over the trail.

He said that often he'd see a tiny piece of root sticking towards the trail and two hours later on his patrol, overgrown green tendrils would cover the place. He said the tendrils would writhe when burnt and there'd be a hiss of some sorts that sounded like the plant was screaming in pain.

He ended his career when one day a stray tendril wrapped itself around his ankle and started dragging him off the trail. He managed to burn the tendril off, but a sharp thorn had found itself embedded in his foot. He plucked it out and continued working, but the following day, he had bulging veins all over his foot. Upon closer inspection, he realized those weren't veins, but tiny tendrils emerging from the

wound where the thorn had pricked him and slowly growing, reaching higher, first towards his ankle, then knee.

He had to have his foot amputated and retired after that with a handsome compensation. When I asked him if he regretted working there, he said he'd give both his feet for this job without a second thought.

Return of the black-eyed people
This story is from one of the intervention members and is related to the story of one of those black-eyed people that I mentioned earlier. The guy who told me this is known to others simply as the Survivor. Apparently he's been on dozens of suicide missions and saw a change of four full teams, being the sole survivor on the squad of every mission. When I met him, he turned out not to be the burly, bald, scar-ridden tough guy I had imagined. Instead he looked like your average Joe - athletic build, eyes that somewhat expressed emotion, approachable personality. He lit a cigarette as he told me his story:

"Heard you met one of those black-eyed people a while ago. Good thing you didn't make the same mistake that one guard made a few years back and let them out. They're nasty when they're off their leashes.

So about that story. A few years back we got a call from HQ to immediately go to the site where you worked and investigate. When we got there, the higher-ups were already there, questioning the guard. More like interrogating. The guard was in a panicked state, rambling about his partner having black eyes. His partner was right there though, and was just as confused as we were.

From his incoherent speech, we figured that the black-eyed entity, who posed as his partner suggested they go out for a quick whiff of fresh air. The guard agreed, even though he had a bad feeling the whole time, as he said. See, that's the one thing that happens often with these black-eyed people. You get a terrible, nagging feeling, but you just can't figure out why or what it is. You also don't realize that they have black eyes for some reason, until it's too late.

So apparently, they went out and the black eyed man just smiled and thanked the guard for escorting him to the exit, before walking away. The rules were never to go out during shift of course, so the guard was put into disciplinary and we were sent to go after the escaped entity.

About an hour later we got intel that he was in a nearby motel. This was bad for us, because what happens is, those things feed on other people. And I don't mean kill them. They do something to you, suck the life out of you and get stronger, while you live out the rest of your days as a vegetable. We hoped that the thing hadn't attacked anyone before we arrived.

The receptionist was just as panicked as the guard and called the cops, so that's how the company found the target. We evacuated everyone under the excuse that there's a dangerous criminal in one of the rooms and went upstairs.

The negotiator knocked on the door, presenting himself as an employee of the motel and asking him to open the door. See the thing is, these guys are not so dangerous if you can get them to open the door willingly. But if they don't... well, let's just say that sending an armored vehicle against them still poses a threat to the driver.

So anyway, the guy on the other side of the door answers, asking who it is. He sounds like a normal human male, nothing suspicious. But after a moment of debating, decides he wants to be left alone. He was probably suspicious, knew that someone would go after him. Anyway, the negotiator steps back, we breach the door and throw in a tear gas grenade. The tear gas itself is so strong, that no one could take even a whiff of it without being affected. Hell, one of my former unit members had a faulty gas mask and started vomiting just two seconds in. But not the black-eyed people.

We burst inside, pointing guns at the guy who looked exactly like the guard we saw earlier, save for the black eyes. And he's just standing there, staring at us through the gas, bemused and unaffected, black eyes reflecting from our flashlights. Without thinking, we open fire and he flinches as the bullets pierce his body, but continues standing.

And then he opens his mouth, so widely that his jaw unhinges and his lips tear at the edges all the way to the ears. All of a sudden instead of human teeth there's a row of spikes and some spindly, spider-like appendages growing out of it's back with a loud, bone-cracking and gurgling sound.

We keep firing, but the thing impales our men one by one with those spider legs. In seconds, only two of us remained and the thing grabbed the other guy and bit his head off whole like it was no more than a piece of tender meat. Somehow I found myself on the ground and without ammo, so I pulled out my handgun and held it trained at the thing. I didn't want to shoot. Somehow I thought that would anger it and I wanted to think of another way, since bullets obviously didn't work.

It turned towards me and got so close that the nuzzle of my gun touched its forehead. It drooled all over the floor, saliva and blood mixed in its mouth and I remember recognizing malice and hunger in its eyes as it stared at me like I was its next meal. I remember contemplating blowing my own brains out before it could do whatever to me.

And then more gunshots from the armored guys who suddenly arrived and the thing jumped out of the window. I quickly got up when the guys stopped shooting and I went for the window, but it was already on the other side of the street, scurrying with its spider legs so quickly that I thought to myself: holy fuck, I'm lucky to be alive. The commander of the armored unit simply approached me and said 'Surprise, surprise, Survivor survives again.'

The black-eyed creature was located weeks later in a remote village, where it had been killing its people one by one in secret, getting stronger. The team that was dispatched to kill it was ordered to keep things quiet, but I doubt that was the case with all the explosives and firepower they used, ha. They practically had to use antitank missiles to kill it. Anyway, they killed the thing finally, but not before it took down two more of our men. And that's that."

He finished his cig by now, so he lit another one. I

remember being amazed at how calm he was talking about his near-death experience at the hands of this monster.

"Do any of your experiences from past missions ever haunt you?" I asked.

He shook his head:

"Nah. If you let it get to you in this line of work, you don't last for too long."

Never, ever walk off trail

A new recruit joined our company recently and was stationed at a park for a while. The place was rarely traversed by people even during daytime, due to dangerous trails and stories about the place being haunted. The rookie told me about his time there and while most nights he said he'd see nothing, there were occasions where he would shit his pants.

For instance, when patrolling, it was a common rule that guards should never walk off trail. The rookie said the first time something happened, it was like this:

He was walking on the trail and all was quiet, when he heard bare footsteps on crunchy leaves in the dark. He stopped and pointed his flashlight, but nothing was there. He took a few more steps and again, more footsteps and the sound of leaves shuffling came from behind him. He turned around again and saw nothing once more.

But then as he moved his flashlight to the right, he saw something that looked like an emaciated man with no clothes, running just out of the reach of the torch beam, disappearing in the dark again. This would happen every time his torch would get in contact with someone – for a split second he'd see a nude person before they ran off, too fast to be tracked or to get a better look.

The rookie continued patrolling, on edge and ready to shoot. When he heard the footsteps again, he turned around and managed to illuminate one of those people. Except this time, the person he illuminated didn't move and instead peeked from behind a tree, as if playing hide and seek. He recognized that it was a woman with long, greasy hair and baggy eyes. She looked like she had been in the wilderness without food and water for a while and on the verge of dying.

They stared at each other for a while and then… she opened her mouth and started screaming. Except it wasn't really screaming, but more of a croaking sound, as if the woman had lost her voice. The rookie fired a few shots and started running and the croaking followed him for a good five minutes, never going quieter or louder. He said it was as if she was maintaining the same distance from him the entire time. She didn't stop even once to breathe in during this entire time, but instead just continued croaking incessantly.

Just before he reached the guardhouse, the croaking was heard right in his ear and then it stopped completely. The emaciated people were gone and he was safe. The rest of the night was quiet. Although I can see it troubles him, he seems determined to continue working. He was transferred from the place recently, so now he works in a more relaxing environment (if you can call it that). From time to time, he wakes up at night when he hears a loud croaking in his ear, he says, but finds no one around.

Upside-down factory

There used to be a guard who worked in a factory. There were no exceptional rules, except don't let anyone in without an ID and don't go inside the working grounds, unless absolutely necessary. The guy described the shifts as completely peaceful, with no strange occurrences. He worked there for about three months, when a factory worker came to him, asking to see the supervisor.

The guard obviously didn't know who the supervisor there was, so he asked the employee's section and went to look for his superior there. Except when he opened the door, nothing was there. Literally no people or machines were inside. The interesting thing though, was the fact that the noise of the machines was so loud, that he couldn't hear anything else. When he looked up at the ceiling, his jaw dropped to the floor.

Up there, on the ceiling, upside down, were people working on their daily duties on the conveyor belts, machines, etc. The guard jerked his head up and down, thinking it was a mirror or an optical illusion, but that wasn't the case, because he couldn't see his own reflection anywhere, nor the machines or people on the floor where he was. It was just then that he realized that the floor he was standing on wasn't a floor at all – it was a ceiling, and neon lights were hanging from the floor up.

The guard suddenly felt dizzy - he described it as staring down from a very tall building - and then he got out of there, not sure what he had just seen. He told the worker that he couldn't find his boss and told him to wait for him or find him himself. Everything went down normally from there., the superior came and went, etc.

The guard continued working and is still there, as far as I'm aware.

The orphanage

There was a guard who worked in an orphanage. On
any daily basis working in an orphanage would take a
mental toll on its staff members, so you can imagine
why no one wanted to fill the spot when HQ gave
information of a vacant position there. The guard who
got the job there had been jobless for a while and was
aware of the potential risks, but was in desperate need
for a job.

The rules were simple. Stay on the orphanage
grounds and let the caretakers do their job. At 9 am
every morning, the orphans would all gather in a big
room. From there, the guards had to put on thermal
goggles and inspect every orphan. If any of them
didn't emit any heat while the goggles were on – in
other words, if the goggles showed the orphan being
devoid of the colors which showed bodily
temperature – they were to be shot on sight.

The guard said everything was fine for a while and
then one day he saw something wrong with one of the
orphans. All the others were shown as yellow, red and
green with the thermals, whereas this one boy was
completely colorless.

The guard was caught off guard (no pun intended)
and instead of following direct orders to just shoot the
kid, he informed his partner. When the partner double
checked, he immediately pointed his gun and shot the
kid directly in the eye. There was widespread panic as
the other kids ran around and the caretakers tried
calming them down. The partner scolded the guard
for not shooting right away. The guard told me that he

had started to feel sick witnessing a child get shot right in front of him, until the next thing that happened.

The kid who was shot started writhing on the ground and producing this high-pitched scream that sounded like a rat being burned alive. The guard described the kid literally melting, until all that was left of him was a steaming red, gooey substance on the ground. He asked what the fuck that was and his partner explained.

He first showed him some pictures of kids, except they weren't kids. They had completely white eyes, pale skin covered in purple veins and sharp teeth. Some of them were slightly creepier, with elongated necks, emaciated extremities or unnaturally hunched backs. Apparently, these creatures find their ways into the orphanage, taking the appearances of normal children and patiently await for a naive family to adopt them. In most cases, when that happens, the parents are found tragically dead some time later and the kid is placed back into the orphanage for a new family.

It's unknown how widespread those creatures are, but one thing's for sure – this isn't the only orphanage where they were spotted.

Evil Santa

For Christmas, all the guards in the office where I work – except intervention - get a day off. Doesn't matter what shift you're doing, but by 5 pm on the 24th, you need to be out of the office. One of the guards offered to stay one year, stating that he and his wife were in a fight and he didn't mind doing a little overtime. HQ wouldn't even hear about it and threatened to fire him if he was found on the grounds after the aforementioned time.

I figured it's just their way of saving up some money and since intervention is basically always on rotation, it made logical sense to me. It wasn't until an intervention member told what was really going on that I got the big picture. Here's what he told me:

"Christmas is supposed to be a really happy time for everyone. You go home, spend time with the family, that sort of thing. But over here, it's one of the worst days of the year. Intervention members are fighting over each other who's going to take paid time off for Christmas Eve. I don't blame them. They know what comes for Christmas and it terrifies them."

He took a long pause, staring into nothingness, as if remembering something, before continuing:

"They put four units of intervention in the office for Christmas Eve. Crazy, huh? We usually have just one unit and that's only in case of an emergency. But for Christmas, something strange comes around. The first time I saw it was four years ago and back then we only had one one unit stationed.

It was my first year in the unit and as we sat there in the comms room, everybody seemed on edge, glancing at the clock every few minutes. I didn't understand it, but figured they were just irritated that they weren't with their families. 11:50 pm comes and the unit leader says simply 'let's move'. I didn't know what this was about, so I just followed my squad.

You know that building that you're never supposed to enter, no matter what you see, building 4? Well we went inside there and the leader led us straight into one of the staff resting rooms, which had a huge fireplace in it. Before I knew what was going on, everybody was pointing their guns at the fireplace and the squad leader looked at me and told me to shoot as soon as I saw something. I was a little nervous, to say the least, but followed my orders and tried to stay calm. In this line of work, if you lose your cool for even a second, you're a dead man.

So anyway, we waited with our guns trained on the fireplace. Everything was silent at first. I heard my watch beep to indicate it was midnight and as if on cue, I heard it – some kind of noise coming from above. I thought it was coming from the ceiling and pointed my gun up, but the commander yelled at me to keep my gun pointed at the fireplace. The scratching from above got louder, as if whatever was there was going down the chimney. And then there was something that sounded like a thud, right from inside the fireplace. And then I heard something that still chills me to the bone when I remember it.

You know how Santa has his trademark 'ho ho ho' laughter? Well we heard that, a very slow ho, ho, ho. Except it didn't sound human. It was as if there were five people saying it at the same time, all with different tones, but perfectly synchronized. We heard another thud before another demonic ho ho ho.

And then a hand came out from inside the fireplace, a skinny, pale, wrinkled up hand, which grabbed the side of the fireplace, as if to get a better grip. You could clearly see that this... thing... wore Santa's clothes, but the sleeve seemed old and dirty. I saw something that looked like additional fingers coming out of its wrist, but they weren't moving like the ones on the hand.

It all happened so fast, but as soon as the hand appeared, everybody started shooting. In a second or so, this creature impersonating Santa popped out for a split second and I saw a shriveled, pale creature with a dirty grey beard and red eyes. I thought it was my imagination, but I was later able to confirm that this thing hands dozens of limp hands, just sticking out of various parts of its body, some of them as full-grown arms.

Anyway, in that split second, Santa grabbed one of our members in a big, blood-stained bag and just like that disappeared back into the fireplace. The commander gave us the order to cease fire and so we did. We listened as our bagged teammate screamed in horror, while Santa dragged him through the chimney. Before he left, he gave us one final, mocking ho ho ho' leaving us in complete silence.

We never saw our teammate again.

Year after year, this thing has been coming back on Christmas Eve and HQ has tried various methods to stop it. Automated turrets, traps, etc. One year they even put clasps on the floor, to hold the unit members from being snatched away. The guy who got bagged that year – the only thing left of him were his feet, still clasped to the floor.

Why don't we just leave it be, you may ask. Well if we do, this thing will get out and bag someone else instead. Someone suggested once to just leave some low-life scum from prison as tribute every Christmas to this creature, so they may start doing that starting next year, if they can pull the right strings.

But one thing is for sure, though. It always comes back. And each time it does, it has more hands coming out of its body."

Mannequins

There was a place where I was stationed for two months, which served as a warehouse of some sort. The warehouse itself was made for mannequins and simply consisted of one big room, filled with hundreds of mannequins, which were no longer in use. I was to work alone there in the shifts, so the senior guard who was about to retire took me for a tour around the place.

He gave me a flashlight and told me to follow him. Now, going through a room full of mannequins at night is creepy enough as it is, but with the quirks that come with our company, it's even worse. The warehouse itself was so crammed with mannequins, that there were makeshift aisles between them, specifically made so that guards could take them as patrolling routes.

"Get your gun ready and keep the safety off." The senior guard told me.

It immediately put me on edge, but he seemed pretty calm and he had been working there for the past six years, so I figured he knew what he was doing.

"This can be a nasty place, if you're not careful." He said "One slip-up and you're done for. Tell me, what do you see with your flashlight?"

I scanned the row of mannequins, checking each one of them out carefully. Some were missing heads, others were missing arms or hands, or were just dirty and overused. Other than that, they seemed like normal mannequins.

"Nothing." I said.

"Yep. Press the button on the back of your flashlight." The senior guard said.

I did as he ordered and instead of the regular light, my flashlight started emitting a blacklight. He told me to scan the area again. I slowly moved my flashlight from left to right, illuminating the mannequins with purple light. Everything seemed normal at first. And then my heart jumped into my throat when I stopped the light on one female mannequin which was different. It was in a regular standing position, with one hand up, as if explaining something, but that wasn't the odd thing. The mannequin wasn't really a mannequin. The crude body shape and the separations between joints which make a mannequin distinct were gone and I was instead looking at a realistic, human woman in old, tattered clothes.

As soon as the blacklight reached her face, she shielded her eyes and then started screaming like a banshee, showing off rows of sharp teeth. I pointed my gun at the thing, but before I could fire, the senior guard already put a bullet between the woman's eyes. Instantly, her head fell off and I was once again looking at a motionless mannequin. She was still in her screaming position, with arms and legs spread, but her head was gone, as it rolled somewhere in the background.

"Like I said. Nasty place." He said "Always use your

blacklight and check every one of them. They are really sneaky. See that one there?"

He pointed his flashlight towards one male mannequin among the crowd, which was in the company's security uniform and missing an arm.

"That was George, the guy who worked here before me." He said.

"What?" I asked.

"Apparently he got a little drunk before the shift and when I arrived, he was like this. On the floor, all... mannequinized... missing an arm. There were a few other mannequins around him, in positions that suggested he was ambushed and killed by them. We're strictly forbidden from touching or moving any of them, so there's no way he managed to put them there in such an elaborate position, especially given the fact that he was so wasted."

"Anything else I should know?" I asked.

"Yeah. If you hear footsteps somewhere, it means you may have missed one of them and now it's trying to ambush you. It's really important that you retrace your steps if that happens and find where it's hiding. It's never going to move in plain sight, unless you point the blacklight at it. You may hear footsteps and as soon as you turn around, everything will be still and quiet. You'll look at the mannequins, sure that you saw them in different positions and postures a minute ago, or they will seem closer to you, but you won't be able to put your finger on it. In that case it's better to be safe than sorry. Go back, check them all out once more and shoot the one that looks human. Just one bullet in the torso or head, your choice. They're pretty fragile."

We had to shoot three more mannequins by the end of the sweep and once we were done, he said:

"Oh, they may sometimes beg you to spare them, pretend they don't know how they got there and so on. If they do that, it means they are trying to distract you and another one may be sneaking up on you. In that case it's best to shoot the pleading fucker and run to the nearest corner. From there, slowly scan the area once more. Again, one slip-up and you're done for. But luckily, you only need to do one sweep per night."

"Are there always mannequins to shoot?"

He nodded:

"The best I got so far was two in a night. The worst… can't count."

Special zoo

One guy from the company works in a zoo of some
sorts, but as far as I'm aware, it isn't a zoo which is
open to the public. His primary job is to feed the
animals once a night and make sure all cages and
enclosures are secure along the way. Here's the thing
– he never saw the animals there, because the cages
are covered on all sides, making it impossible to peer
inside. The guard would carry a bucket full of meat
(some of it rotten) and he carried around a piece of
paper which said which meat goes into which cage.

For one cage however, he had to take a live, sedated
pig and lead it to a slide, which dropped directly into
the cage. He described that just seconds after the pig
was delivered, he'd hear a deep growl and the pig
would begin screaming in agony. Loud sounds of
crunching and rabid chewing came from inside the
cage for a few minutes after that. The pig would stop
screaming within the first minute.

The second strict rule he has to follow is to patrol the
area three times during the night and make sure all
locks are secure tightly, calling the repairman for
replacement if they so much as had their paint
scratched. If he was to see any external damage on
the cages, like broken bars, busted walls, etc., he was
to remain as still as possible and just move his hand
enough to radio HQ by uttering the code 10-98. He
was to remain as still as possible until the intervention
unit arrived and escorted him out of there.

He never got into that situation though, but he did feel
on edge the first few shifts, because he'd often hear

growling, thrashing, banging on the bars, etc. Despite not being able to see him, he was sure the animals knew exactly where he was at all times, because he could hear them following him alongside the cage when he patrolled.

He also said he'd often have armored units arrive in APCs, armed to the teeth, escorting something out in a cage so secure, that C4 couldn't get through it. They'd place the animal in its enclosure and leave the place without a word. I asked him what exactly is being guarded there and he shrugged, saying:

"Well I can tell you one thing for sure. Whatever it is, it's no fucking cougar."

Bad prank

A guard by the name of Michael used to work in an abandoned hotel. There were three other guards in the shift with him, each guard covering one floor. They had radios to keep each other company and generally nothing ever happened in the hotel. Michael told me about the night when he decided to quit the job in the middle of his shift.

It was around 2 am in the morning and he was patrolling around the second floor, checking each room. The rule was that if they found anyone or anything in any of the rooms, or even heard any noise, they were to go back to the reception and call the intervention unit. So anyway, Michael went about his patrol normally, when he suddenly heard a noise coming from the bathroom in room 204. He radioed it in to his coworkers, but no one responded. He tried multiple times, but it was as if the line was dead.

Not wanting to go all the way back to the reception and being curious about the noise, he slowly approached and opened the bathroom. He saw one of the guards there, standing in front of the mirror – guard Sean from floor 3, to be precise. Michael asked him if he's okay, but Sean just stood there, staring at the mirror and what Michael described as twitching his shoulder and head from time to time. When Michael grabbed him by the shoulder, Sean turned around and made his coworker scream in horror.

Apparently, Sean's face was completely distorted, as if his skin was stretched to the side of his face. Michael said that it looked like Sean was wearing a leather mask which he failed to put on his face properly and it was just sitting there sideways. Sean staggered towards Michael with an outreached arm, muttering something incoherent in a muffled tone, since his mouth was practically where his cheek was, revealing the sides of his teeth.

Michael ran out of there, slamming the door to 204 shut and tumbling down the stairs to the reception. When he got there, he tried radioing his coworkers again, but got only a muffled groan as a response over the radio. He panicked and picked up the phone to call intervention, when the door suddenly burst open. Two of his coworkers were there, laughing their asses off. Michael asked them what was so funny and they said it was all just a prank to scare him. He put the phone down and breathed a sigh of relief.

He didn't get angry and even commended them on a job well done, putting such a realistic mask on Sean. This is when his two coworkers gave each other a weird glare. When Michael asked them what was wrong, one of them simply said:

"Sean wasn't in on the prank."

It was then that they realized that Sean was unresponsive on the radio. Michael described being in sort of a trance from that moment. He doesn't clearly remember it, but his coworkers tried radioing Sean and when he didn't respond, they called the intervention unit. The unit went to investigate and after hearing gunshots coming from the second floor, Michael simply left the company belongings on the counter of the reception and left through the front door, never to come back again.

THE SURVIVOR

Part 1

I held my trusty assault rifle with a light grip, leaning back against the inside of the vehicle. I couldn't see where we were going, but the ride was pretty smooth, so I figured we were at least not going to an overly remote area. It's been a while since my last mission and this long drive oddly reminded me of my first intervention with the unit. I was nervous back then and my commander noticed that, so he told me to pull myself together, because in this line of work, one moment of panic could get your team members – or yourself - killed. I listened to him and focused as best I could and in the end the mission was a success, with no incurred losses. I've been on countless missions since and as I now rode in the APC, I felt nothing similar to that rookie-like nervousness like on my first mission.

"We'll be there in around five minutes, get ready." The driver said from the front.

"Roger that." Unit leader Jones said and turned to us "Safeties off and let's go over the mission details once more."

I took my safety off as he commanded and returned to my previous leaning position, now holding my rifle a little tighter. The unit leader and my other two team members - Bryans and Torres - were leaning forward, visibly on edge.

"So, what do we know?" Bryans asked.

The unit leader placed the butt of his gun on the floor, pointing it upwards and said:

"We've had radio silence from the guards at the campus for over two hours now. There's five of them and they're supposed to report every hour to HQ. For some reason though, all five of them went radio silent at the same time and haven't been responsive since."

"It's almost 2 am on a Friday night." Torres shrugged "Maybe they just fell asleep or got drunk. HQ could have given them another hour or so, before they started bothering us."

"There's a reason for them reporting so frequently, Torres." The unit leader rebutted "The college campus is a highly sensitive area and as soon as there's something suspicious going on there, HQ needs to take action. And if all five of them somehow did fall asleep at the same time or showed up drunk for duty, they'll have a lot more to worry about than just losing their jobs."

"So, what's our objective?" I asked calmly, causing the other unit members to jerk their heads towards me.

Jones said:

"Head to the nearest guardhouse near the parking lot and reckon the situation. If the guard is there, get intel on what happened. If he's not, we'll have to go in."

"Are we getting support from any other units?" I asked.

Jones shook his head:

"There's not enough manpower right now. Team Alpha is out on another mission and the other teams are too crucial for the areas they've been assigned to. They need to be there in case there's an incident."

"But the campus is huge. How the fuck are we supposed to investigate the whole place?" Torres asked.

The truck slowed down and then halted to a stop. The driver killed the engine, instantly shrouding us in complete silence.

"We're here." He said.

The unit leader looked at Torres and said:

"That's our job."

The backdoor of the APC swung open, street lights instantly bathing the vehicle interior in orange light. I got out after my team members and scanned the area. We were in parking lot, which was all but empty, save for four parked vehicles, which I assumed belonged to the college guards and some other night staff. There was a tollgate right next to a guardhouse in front of us, surrounded by a tall fence on both sides, stretching far beyond our view. This marked the entrance to the campus. The fence made it seem more like a prison than a college, which made me wonder if that was the impression they were trying to give.

The inside of the actual campus was coupled with tall trees, various paved paths and university buildings, while the outside area was surrounded by thick woods, making the college completely cut off from civilization. There was a single road leading through the woods back into the city and it took us around twenty minutes to arrive from HQ to the university grounds, so a lot could have happened in the meantime.

I glanced at the guardhouse and realized it was empty, despite the lights being left on.

"No time to waste, let's move." Jones said and took point.

He raised his rifle before even reaching the tollgate, ready to shoot. The unit was authorized to use lethal force, in case we thought we were in any danger and more often than not, we returned home with fewer bullets than in the beginning of the mission. The rest of us followed the leader, getting into formation and carefully observing our surroundings. As we got closer to the guardhouse, we realized that something was very wrong over there. The four of us entered the guardhouse, still gripping our rifles firmly.

The handset of the phone dangled off its cord on the table, slowly swinging back and forth in steady motion, indicating that someone had been there just recently. The chair was overturned on the floor and there were fresh blood stains on it and on the floor next to it. Upon closer inspection, I realized there was blood on the phone handset as well, in the form of bloody fingerprints. The amount of blood in the room didn't seem like the type of injury you get cutting yourself on a tuna can while having a meal, so we knew right there and then that we were in for a mess on our hands.

"The fuck happened here?" Torres asked.

Jones lowered his rifle, looking around the room. I approached the desk and leaned in to take a look at the monitor which had the camera feed. There was a blood stain on the screen, covering one feed partially. From the dozens of camera feeds on the screen, it became apparent that the whole university was being monitored. I looked around and saw no movement on any of the cameras, but as I scanned through, I saw one of the guards on the feed marked as Lab – East, strewn on the floor of the hallway, on his back, with arms and legs spread. Dark liquid stained the floor beneath him.

"Damn, that's the guard assigned to secure the Eastern perimeter of the campus." Bryans said tonelessly.

Just then, I saw movement on one of the cameras covering the science building. It was one of the guards, sprinting through the hallway. Although the footage was not clear on this particular camera, the guard was visibly scared for his life based on his body language – he ran in a frantic, panicked motion by flailing his arms and taking unsteady steps, glanced over his shoulder every second or so, etc. When he rounded the corner, he stopped and peeked around and then instantly backed away in terror. He opened one of the lockers and quickly hid inside.

A few seconds later, someone else appeared on the same feed. I couldn't tell who it was though, because as soon as he did, the camera started acting up, making it almost impossible to see anything. The strange thing was, everything else on the camera seemed fine, but wherever the person moved, the area would become pixeled and grainy just in that particular area. The camera continued acting up for at least a whole minute, as the person made his way randomly around the hallway. Our unit stared, transfixed in anticipation.

Eventually, the person walked off the visibility of the camera and the feed returned back to normal, as we were faced again with the view of lockers. Another half a minute or so later, the guard emerged from his locker timidly, looking in both directions. He quietly closed the locker door. Jones pressed the button on his radio and said as quietly as possible:

"This is the special response unit, is anybody out there?"

The guard seemed to notice this, as he grabbed his radio and said something into it. Jones waited for a moment, but no response came back. He tried asking again if anyone out there heard him. Nothing but silence. And then something came through. At first, it was a second or so of static and then we heard a male voice breaking up:

"Thi... ard from.... Do... an... science bui..."

"Repeat that last, you cut off. Where are you?" Jones asked sternly.

".... go an... th... ence building..."

Just then, a loud, ear-piercing, animalistic shriek came from the other end of the radio, so sharp and long that I felt shivers running down my spine, even at this distance. The guard on the camera shot his head in the direction down the hallway and started running again, faster and more panicked than before. "This is the response unit leader. You there, in the science building, can you hear me?!"

There was another staticky noise, coupled with the sound of broken up panting and that same monstrous screeching, before it went silent completely. The cameras started acting up at the same time as well and we were unable to see where the guard had run off to and what was chasing him. We stared at the motionless, quiet camera feed for a minute or so, before I finally turned away from the screen.

"He mentioned the science building." I said "We should check that place out, first."

"We might wanna call for some backup." Torres stated.

"You know the drill." Jones said "No backup until we confirm what we're up against. Bryans, you stay here and monitor the feed. Keep us informed of any movement, got it?"

"Roger that." Bryans nodded and immediately lifted the chair and sat by the desk.

"The two of you, you're coming with me. We gotta see if we can save that other guard and get some intel from him." Jones said.

We quickly checked out the map on the wall of the guardhouse, which showed where each point of interest in the campus was located. The science building was pretty close to the guardhouse itself, to our relief, since the campus was enormous.

"Let's move." Jones said and opened the door.
The outside was unnervingly quiet as we made our way there, even the chirping of birds and insects not being heard, leaving us with nothing but the sound of our own boots echoing on pavement. With our years of training and the kinds of missions we've been on before, we knew better than to let our guard down, so I kept an eye on the left side, while Torres did the same on the right side. Jones took point and made sure nothing unexpected jumped in front of us. The science building stood in front of us, a silent behemoth, four floors tall. Some of the classrooms still had lights on, but most of them were engulfed in pitch darkness.
"Bryans, anything moving in there?" Jones asked as we neared the statue of a prominent scientist in front of the building.
"Negative. No sign of the guard either." Bryans' voice came over in a reply.
"Alright, let's move."
Jones opened the front door and the three of us burst inside, pointing our guns with flashlights in various directions, illuminating the hallway and lockers in front. As soon as we stepped inside the building, the air suddenly felt extremely heavy, like stepping from a cold room into a sauna. Not physically, mind you, but in some way I can't really explain to this day. I usually didn't feel anything except adrenaline on missions like these, but for some reason this time every fiber of my being was screaming at me to get out of there.

I couldn't do that, however. I had a mission to complete and that guard needed rescuing. The unit leader took point and I followed him, as he motioned for us stay close, quietly taking step by step forward, never letting his guard down. The general rule for the unit was to avoid speaking while on a mission, unless it was absolutely safe, since it could give away our position, so Jones reverted to hand signals instead. We hadn't made it halfway down the hallway when a loud bang resounded somewhere in the distance. Jones raised his hand to signal to us to stop. We stood in silence with our rifles raised, pointing them at the far end of the hallway, covering both the left and right side where the corridor forked. And then we saw something run past us from left to right, with an insanely quick batter of barefoot footsteps, disappearing around the corner. I'm not even sure that the word run is the right one in this case, because whatever it was, ran past us was so quickly, that you could literally miss it if you blinked.

"What the fuck was that?" Torres asked, pointing his gun left and right in a confused manner.

We stared without blinking, trigger fingers at the ready. Jones gently pressed the radio button and asked:

"Bryans, see anything?"

There was a sound of static coming from the other end.

"Bryans." Jones repeated, but no response came.

He looked genuinely unsure what the next best approach should be, but after a moment of contemplation, he signaled for us to follow him. He pointed his gun around the corner where that fast thing had disappeared and then, I honestly don't know what happened next. There was a loud screech similar to the one we heard on the radio, which oddly reminded of skidding car tires, but this time it was fuller of audible malice and anger. Jones started firing, filling my ears with ringing noise, mixed with the echoing bangs of gunfire.

This all lasted for two seconds tops, because as soon as Jones started firing and before Torres and I could reach him, that thing from before flew back the way it came as quickly as it did before, but this time it took Jones along with it, making the both of them disappear around the corner, just like that, in a split second. It all happened so quickly, that we saw Jones' rifle fall out of thin air onto the ground with a loud clank.

Torres ran to the gun and pointed his own gun in the direction where the leader was taken. I followed closely behind, scanning the hallway along with him. It was empty. Rows of lockers on both sides and a hallway which ended in consuming darkness, our flashlights unable to illuminate it all the way to the end. But other than the darkness, there was nothing.

"Commander!" Torres called out into the dark. Another scream echoed somewhere in the distance, this time much longer, filling me with primordial fear. I heard that same sound of bare feet thudding on the floor, rapidly approaching us and I knew that we had to get out of there.

"Torres, we gotta get the fuck out, now!"

I turned back towards the exit along with Torres and we started sprinting down the hallway. The scream resounded again, this time right in my ear and I heard a thump and a yelp, realizing Torres had somehow tripped and fallen. I turned back to help him and to my horror, saw him getting dragged down the hallway by his foot, almost as quickly as Jones, but slowly enough for me to see his face full of fear, as he reached out towards me in vain and screamed futilely. I opened fire at whatever could have been dragging him, even though I saw nothing in the darkness and just before he disappeared around the corner, I saw Torres turn on his back while still being dragged and shoot at his captor. The shooting lasted for a few seconds, before it abruptly stopped.

I stood there with my rifle pointed down the hallway, breathing heavily, the beam of my flashlight steadily going up and down. I couldn't process what the fuck just happened. And then a noise snapped me back from my trance into reality. It sounded like those same footsteps from before, right around the corner, but this time slow and dragged on the floor intermittently. And it was getting closer.

"It's coming back for you. Hide!" I heard Bryans' panicked voice on the radio.

I couldn't make up my mind. Should I run? Fight? Hide? My flashlight illuminated an elongated, pale hand reaching out and grabbing around the corner of the wall with boney fingers that had jagged, dirty nails. I then heard a wheezing noise from around the corner, as if the creature had trouble breathing, while dragging its feet heavily on the ground.

My instincts kicked in and I suddenly knew better than to try and fight this thing face to face, so I ran to the nearest classroom and closed the door behind me as silently as I could, ducking under just in time to hear the footsteps and wheezing get louder and stop in front of the door.

I held the door firmly with my shoulder, trying not to make any movements, holding my breath. The only thing separating me from most likely a sure death was this door and the wheezing was right on the other side of it, so close that I could practically smell the monster's rotted breath even through the small crack under the door. It sniffed the air curiously, wheezing between sniffs. Gradually, the heavy dragging of the creature's feet started again and it began to fade away along with the wheezing. It stopped again and a loud sound was heard outside the classroom, like something metallic scraping another metal surface. More footsteps and wheezing in my direction, but they simply went past the door and gradually faded away. I steadily exhaled in relief, when my radio crackled to life, nearly making me jump out of my own skin:

"They fucked up. Now we're all fucked." It was an unfamiliar voice.

There was a blood-curdling scream down the hall again and a series of rapid footsteps closing in in a matter of seconds, before whatever was out there slammed directly into the classroom door. I almost fell over from the impact, but continued holding the door firmly. It was no use though, since the creature was so strong that it was only a matter of time before it busted the door open.

I tried bracing the door and getting my gun ready to shoot when the creature bursts in, but before I had a chance to do it, there was a loud crash somewhere in the building and the slamming on the door instantly stopped. Another screech ensued right in my ear, followed by an impossibly quick batter of footsteps which seemed to cover insurmountable distance within seconds and fade away completely. Whatever caused that crash got the creature's attention, which worked to my advantage. I wasn't sure how long I had though, so I had to act quickly.

"It's gone now." Bryans' voice came over the radio calmly "You're in the clear."

"Bryans, where the fuck have you been?!" I scolded him and immediately moved to the corner of the classroom to avoid drawing the creature back "What the fuck was that thing? And where are Jones and Torres?"

"I'm sorry." Bryans said over the radio "They're dead. You need to get the hell outta there. I'll call backup."

"Fuck! Is it safe?" I asked.

"There's no one there as far as I can see. Move your fuckin' ass before it comes back!"

I carefully exited the classroom with my gun raised, looking down the hallway and then towards the exit. As soon as I did, I couldn't help but mouth a what the fuck in frustration and bafflement. The metallic handles on the exit door had been twisted together into a knot, making it impossible to open the door. I was stuck in here.

Part 2

"Bryans, come in. Door's barred." I said into the radio, looking over my shoulder.

"What?" Bryans asked a second later.

"The door's fucking barred. That thing twisted the metal handles, I can't get out." I said, more frustrated this time.

A moment of silence, before Bryans finally responded:

"Shit! Alright, listen. There's a back entrance into the building, you'll have to go to the other side."

"Got it. Did you call backup?"

"I did, but their ETA is one hour."

"Are you shitting me?!"

There was a heavy set of footsteps on the floor above, which reminded me to lower my voice. I gripped my gun firmly and waited for them to fade away, before I spoke into the radio again, more quietly this time:

"One hour is too long, we'll all get killed by then! And if this thing gets out, we're fucked!"

"All other units are busy. Look, I told them how serious the situation is and they said they'll send in the armored guys. For now, you just need to get the hell outta there." Bryans said.

"Can't leave. There's someone else still alive, I heard them on the radio just before."

"Yeah, it was probably the guard from before. He's hiding in the basement lab."

"You see him?"

"Yeah, but forget about him, you need to get your ass out of there."

I sighed:

"Negative. Backup is taking too long. Gotta pick him up before that thing gets to him and get some intel."

"Are you out of your mind?!" Bryans' agitated voice came through "Did you even see that thing in there? It took Torres and Jones, you gotta-'

"Where's the creature now?" I interrupted him.

Bryans went silent for a moment, before saying:

"Third floor. I still can't see it clearly, though. Must be causing some interference with the cameras."

"Can you see Torres and Jones anywhere?" I asked.

"No. They were taken off camera views. I doubt they're still alive, though."

"Got it. Gonna pick up the guard, keep me posted on the creature's movement."

"Roger. Out." Bryans said lethargically.

I raised my rifle and started down the hallway slowly, trying to make as little noise as possible. Although the building seemed empty for now, it was so dark even with my flashlight, that it looked like something could jump out in front of me in an instant, especially considering the absurd speed of that creature. I remembered seeing on the map back in the guardhouse that the building's stairs were on the West side, so I turned left.

It worked out well, because in the back of my mind I wanted to take the path where I saw Jones and Torres disappear, in hopes to at least find their bodies, if nothing else. I was just about to turn around the corner, when I saw blood stains on the floor. They went in a straight line across the floor and ended out of my flashlight's reach. I slowly followed the trail, keeping a lookout in front for that creature's sudden return. Then the blood trail suddenly ended and my flashlight instead illuminated a boot. I got closer and realized there was an entire body there, or whatever was left of it.

The body was cut in the middle and literally split in half, from the crotch all the way up to the abdomen. No, more like ripped. The way the legs were spread in an unnatural way indicated that the creature may have grabbed the victim by the legs and ripped the body apart, as incredible as it sounded. But then again, seeing the speed of movement of the creature that got my teammates, it didn't seem so far-fetched.

A large pool of blood and spilled guts decorated the floor around the body. I recognized the uniform and my heart sank when I pointed the flashlight at the victim's face. Jones' eyes stared blankly at the ceiling, his mouth agape in terror, trickles of dried blood on the side of his face.

"Fuck. Bryans, do you read me?" I said into the radio.

"Go ahead." Bryans said.

"I found Jones. He's dead." I knelt down for a better view.

Whatever the hell this thing was, it was capable of doing some serious damage.

"Shit. The creature got him?" Bryans asked.

"I don't know. He's been ripped in half, so whatever did this isn't fucking around."

"Fuck, man. Any sign of Torres?"

"Not that I can see. I'll let you know if I find any signs of him."

I proceeded through the hallway and just then heard a loud crash somewhere on my floor. I pointed my gun at the source of the sound, realizing it must have come from one of the nearby classrooms. The cameras didn't cover any of the classrooms, so I knew asking Bryans if he could see anything would be pointless. I stood frozen for a long moment, waiting to see if more sounds would come from the classroom. Another crash, but this time from somewhere upstairs.

I knew I wouldn't feel safe with something potentially tailing me from behind, so I decided that the best course of action would be checking it out. I approached the door and reached for the knob, gently grabbing it. As slowly as I could, I turned it and pushed the door. It creaked in an alarmingly loud manner, revealing an empty classroom in front. I stepped inside, carefully observing my surroundings when I saw something move behind the teacher's desk with the corner of my eye.

"Don't move!" I pointed my gun to the source.

"Whoa, don't shoot!" A familiar face popped out from under the desk, raising one hand up.

I lowered my gun and breathed a sigh of relief.

"Torres." I said "You made it. Why didn't you use your comms?"

Torres stood up and approached me, glancing over my shoulder:

"Where's that thing? Is it still around?"

"You didn't answer my question." I sternly said.

He looked at me and said:

"That thing busted my radio. I could hear you guys, but couldn't talk back."

"I see. Listen, that guard from before is in the basement. We gotta pick him up and evacuate."

"Pick him up? Are you out of your mind?" He scoffed.

Torres got inches close to my face and said:

"Did you fucking see what that thing did to Jones? Our bullets barely did anything to it. This situation is bigger than the two of us."

"You can leave if you want, Torres. But I need to get intel from him. We don't know how serious the situation is." I said.

Torres shook his head in disbelief. Just then, another loud crash came from somewhere upstairs and both Torres and I looked at the ceiling. He looked down at me and said:

"Alright, fine. Let's get the intel from the guard, but after we do that, we get out, all of us, no heroics. Got it?"

"Understood." I nodded.

Torres took point and I contacted Bryans in the meantime:

"Bryans, I found Torres, he's alive."

"Seriously?" Bryans said "That's great. Now pick up the guard and get outta there, that thing is back on the second floor now."

"Roger."

Torres and I went downstairs to the basement and I felt a lot better now that I had another teammate on my side again. Although I survived lots of missions as the last man standing, a lot of it was luck-based and as much as I hated thinking this way, it felt relieving to have someone who could potentially take the heat off you or be in the center of attention for hostiles. I didn't even think about it until later, but had it been me that the monster grabbed instead of Jones, I wouldn't be here writing this right now. Despite all of this, the mission always came first and we were trained not to think about the potential risks for our lives, otherwise we could lose our cool and fail the mission or get killed.

I saw the sign *LAB* above the door at the end of the basement, so Torres and I took positions to breach it. He kicked the door down and I burst inside with my gun raised, closely followed by my partner. The lab was relatively small, a few rows of desks, a big shelf full of various chemicals and a closet. The room itself had a window near the top, which led directly outside. It was obvious that the only possible hiding post for the guard was the closet.

"Come out, we're with the company." I said, pointing my gun at the closet.

Nothing happened.

"Hey, don't make us fucking drag your ass out here." Torres said.

A moment later, a voice came from the closet:

"Alright, alright, calm down." The door opened and the guard we saw on the cameras stepped forward. He was very young, in his early twenties maybe, and looked pale as a sheet of paper, his eyes wide in fear. "You're here to rescue me?" He asked.

"Yeah. Tell us what happened so we can get out of here." I answered.

"Wait, no. We can't leave, yet. Not until we kill the Mother in the Biology and Genetics Study Center." The guard quickly recited.

"What are you talking about?" Torres asked.

"You've seen that thing out there, right? There's more of them. The small ones aren't that dangerous. But they grow fast and their skin becomes tough as hell. And they're all over the campus. They already killed the other four guards."

"All the more reason for us to get out and let the big guys handle it. They'll be here in about an hour. Let's move." I said and was about to get going, when the guard spoke again.

"You don't understand. We can't wait for backup. By the time they come, these things will be all over the place in even greater numbers. They reproduce extremely quickly and if we don't stop it, it's not just the campus that's going to be in trouble."

Torres and I gave each other contemptuous glances, before we looked back at the guard.

"Tell us everything." I said.

The guard started pacing around and said:

"One of the professors here ran a project with his assistant and a group of volunteering students. It was an extremely secretive project, so much that the students were threatened they'd get kicked out of school for disclosing any information. It was called the Fertility Project."

"So, how do you know about it, then?"

"Because the experiment's gone wrong and the whole thing is now out of control. Listen, we don't have time for this! I'll tell you everything, but right now we gotta get to the Biology Center and-"
A loud sound of glass breaking resounded in the room and a long, emaciated hand reached in through the window. It grabbed the guard by his head and lifted him up from the ground effortlessly. The guard screamed and squirmed, but the hand seemed to grip him firmly like a vice. Torres and I opened fire on the unseen creature and almost as soon as we did, it screeched, similarly to the creature back in the hallway. It instantly let go of the guard, who fell down and scooted away to the opposite wall. The hand pulled back out of the window and a set of footsteps running away was heard just outside. Another scream came, but this one inside the building. Bryans' voice came in:
"It's coming down! Get outta there!"

A second later we heard that same, gut-wrenching set of footsteps, but this one rapidly approaching and the classroom door swung open. In front of us stood a tall, pale, humanoid create. That's the best way I can describe it. It was so tall that I wondered how it got in, since the top of the door frame was way under its head, even though it was hunched over. It had a face which resembled a human's, but was distorted, with tiny, uneven eyes, crooked mouth and a jaw that looked like it was broken in places. Thin, black strands of hair protruded from its head. Its body was thin, emaciated even, so much that I saw its ribs prominently against its stretched skin. The arms were disproportionately long, almost reaching to the ground, with enormous hands at the ends. The legs were equally skinny and ended in large, flat feet that instantly made me wonder how the fuck it could run so quickly.

As soon as the creature got in, it looked to its left, at the guard against the wall. It opened its mouth and screamed, revealing rows of blackened, jagged teeth. It grabbed the guard by his arm, who started screaming as well, and Torres and I opened fire, but the creature barely even flinched from the impact of bullets. Moreover, it looked like the creature's flesh was so hard, that bullets didn't even penetrate its skin. It swung the guard and slammed him on the floor effortlessly, as if he were no more than a bag of feathers. The guard instantly went silent as his head hit the floor, but was still conscious. The creature didn't stop there though, and swung again, slamming the guard again with a sickening crack. It kept doing so, each time leaving a slightly larger stain of blood on the spot it would hit.

By the time it was done with the guard, his skull was dented in and his body a bloody mess of unnaturally twisted extremities. It dropped the guard's body on the floor and then turned its attention to us, letting out another heart-wrenching scream. It charged at me at a speed I couldn't comprehend and grabbed me by my torso, raising me up. I instinctively drew my knife and since it held me close enough, stabbed the fucker in the chest. The knife penetrated its skin easily all the way to the hilt and the monster immediately let me go and screamed even louder this time, flailing its arms frantically around the room. Torres and I kept our rifles trained at it as the creature's scream slowly got weaker, until it stopped altogether and the monster fell on its side, wheezing shallowly. We carefully approached it and before it took its last breath, it looked at me one last time and then closed its eyes. Torres gave it a kick, to see if it would get back up. The creature didn't respond to the kick and instead lay there, motionless.

"Son of a bitch, you did it!" Torres said, lowering his gun.

I knelt down and grabbed my knife, pulling it out with ease, with a squishy sound. The blade was covered in black blood. I was surprised at how soft its skin was around the chest, so to test my theory, I tried stabbing it in the abdomen and sure enough, the knife's tip barely grazed the skin. It felt like trying to stab a piece of rock with a thin layer of leather over it.

"I guess its chest was its only weak spot." I said, examining the wound where I had stabbed it.

"The guard said there's more of them. But the one that broke the window looked smaller." Torres interjected.

"You think so?" I wiped the blade on the monster and stood up.

Bryans' voice came in:

"Guys?! Are you alright?!"

"We're fine." I responded "The guard didn't make it, though. Neutralized the hostile, but there's more of them."

"I know. I see them on the cameras, they're all over the place."

Torres stared at the creature for a moment in silence, until I turned to him and said:

"I know you probably think we should fall back and wait for backup, but we don't have that much time. We need to stop this thing from spreading."

Torres nodded determinately and said:

"You're right. If they really grow as fast as the guard said, imagine what will happen if we have dozens or hundreds of them on our hands."

I contacted Bryans again and said:

"Bryans, we need to find the Biology and Genetics Study Center. Can you see it on the map?"

"Hold on." Bryans said "Yeah, it's just South-West of your position, should be a big blue building. Meet you there."

"Wait, before you do. I need you to contact HQ and ask them about the Fertility Project."

"The Fertility Project? What's that?"

"No time to explain. Do it and meet us in front of the building."

"Roger that."

I gave Torres a pat on his shoulder and turned to the door, saying:

"Let's go kill that Mother."

Part 3

The walk towards the Biology and Genetics Study Center was uneventful. Torres and I thought we heard rustling in the bushes on occasion, but nothing came out after us. When we arrived to the front of the building, I contacted Bryans via comms again:
"Bryans, gimme a sit-rep." I said.
"Just got intel from HQ. On my way to you now." He said.
"Any hostiles around your area?"
"Negative. All clear for now."
Just a minute later, we saw Bryans lightly jogging down the pavement towards us. He stopped in front of us and said:
"Good to see you're both still in one piece. We're in deep shit over here."
"Well, we assumed so." Torres interjected "So, what's going on? HQ better have a damn good reason for keeping us in the dark like this."
Bryans sighed and started:
"They do. The truth is, they have no idea what's going on, either. Here's the full story. The company signed a contract with the college, when professor Richards started the so-called Fertility Project. The purpose of the project was impregnate women who were deemed infertile or unable to bare children for some other reason. But the problem is, HQ has no idea what the fuck these creatures are and neither does the college and they are the ones who funded the project. The project was top secret, so only the relevant info was disclosed to the company."
"Unless it wasn't." I said.
Bryans continued:

"HQ suspects Richards is hiding something. The guards at the campus have pretty mundane duties, except for the guard stationed here in this building. His main job was to prevent anyone from entering it and especially Richards' office, where he kept all his research data. HQ also knows for a fact that the experiments were conducted inside the building, on the basement floor, where only Richards and other project participants had access through his office."

"So, what does HQ want us to do?" I asked.

"Eliminate Richards and destroy his data, along with anything relevant to the project, including the entire experimental lab. That's a direct order given by the client, or should I say the college, to the company."

"How the fuck do we do that?" Torres asked.

"Glad you asked." Bryans smiled and reached out behind his back.

He brought forth a C4 explosive, which he promptly put back.

"Alright, let's move then." I said.

We breached the door and found ourselves in a similar hallway to the one in the science building, but this one was a lot dirtier. The floor seemed to be covered in some sort of greenish-brown muck. It was dry in most places, but still sticky and wet in some.

"Richards' office is on this floor, West side." Bryans said.

He didn't even finish that sentence, when we heard a sudden scream somewhere in the building. Out of the corner at the end of the hallway, a silhouette peeked its head, staring curiously at us. The creature then came into full view and what I saw resembled that of the big creature that had killed Jones and the security guard. Except it was a lot smaller, the size of a toddler perhaps. It screamed similarly to its adult version, the sound of screeching car tires permeating the building, but with a lot less intensity and noise. We managed to silence it halfway through its screech with just a few bullets, but we were too late. Dozens of screams filled the building and instantly, on our floor and the ones above, we heard hundreds of tiny footsteps running all over the place. In seconds, they started to appear from around the corner down the hallway, dozens of creatures like the one we just killed and they all shrieked as they ran towards us. My team and I opened fire immediately and all of them fell pretty easily, unlike the big one we saw back in the science building. More and more kept showing up, closing in, as the building was filled with a cacophony of bullets being fired and the creatures' blood-curdling screams.

I was about to shout to my teammates to fall back, afraid we'd run out of ammo, but just as quickly as the screams started, they abated and only a few stragglers remained, running over the corpses of their brothers (or sisters), trying to reach us, despite not ever having a chance of doing so. Torres shot the final one and the screams completely stopped along with the bullets, filling the building with unnerving silence.

"See any more of them?" I asked, not putting my gun down.

"That's all of them." Bryans said as he reloaded. The hallway was filled with dozens of bullet-riddled corpses of child-sized, freakish monsters strewn over each other, the green much mixed with their dark blood, making the gruesome scene look like a mass tomb.

"Juveniles." Torres remarked.

Carefully, we stepped over the bodies and proceeded to the West part of the building, into Richards' office, which ostentatiously contrasted the rest of the building, with expensive-looking drinks in the cabinet, trophies on the walls, etc. There was an electronic door on the other side of the room behind the desk, which led downstairs and it had a gaping hole in it, the dent protruding towards the office, indicating that the creatures must have broken out from the inside. In the corner of the room against the wall was the unmistakably mutilated body of Richards.

"That our guy?" I asked.

"Looks like it." Torres said as he knelt down to inspect him "No reason for anybody else to be here." There was a PC on the desk and despite the room being in a mess and the monitor being overturned, it still worked. I sat by the desk and flipped the monitor upright. The PC was unlocked and displayed the desktop screen.

"Really? Not even a password?" Torres asked.

"I guess he didn't have time to log out." Bryans said.

There was a folder right in the middle of the desktop called FP. The Fertility Project? I double clicked it and there were various files inside, including documents. I opened the first one and it said:

THE FERTILITY PROJECT

The purpose of the project is to fertilize females which were otherwise deemed infertile. The project is still in its early stages and purely experimental and therefore does not guarantee any results.

Furthermore, adverse effects have not been 100% eliminated and may be visible in some subjects. Due to this, all participants (including test subjects) are under strict obligation to sign an NDA, under risk of 'federal violation' in case they disclose any sensitive information.

The subjects consist of five women between the ages of 20-28, who are unable to bare children and signed up as volunteers. They will remain in the facility for the duration of the project (three months if unsuccessful, twelve months if able to conceive).

During this time, my assistant and the twelve students who volunteered for the project will run daily tests on the subjects. The entire project has been funded by the college.

"Well I'll be." Bryans said "I wonder what happened to those women."

I opened the next document, which had a timeline of the events. It said:

Day 1: Subjects introduced to facility. Each subject injected with a different strain of [REDACTED]. Changes should occur within 14 days.

Day 2: No visible changes.

Day 7: Subject 2 and Subject 4 have unexpectedly died overnight. I have disposed of their bodies and told the other participants that they resigned from the project and were let go.

Day 9: Out of the five subjects, two (Subject 1 and Subject 3) were tested positive for pregnancy. This is a breakthrough in science and could solve the life-long problem of infertility among married couples and otherwise.

Day 21: Pregnant subjects' weight has rapidly increased, along with the size of the abdomen. The pregnancy seems to be progressing a lot faster than we anticipated, as the ultrasound is displaying the growth of the fetus, the likes of which was not expected to be seen before the third trimester.

Day 26: Subject 1 has died at approximately 01:03 am. The rapid growth of the baby has gone out of hand as the subject's stomach was ripped open from the inside. The baby died shortly after and upon examination, physical deformities became apparent.

There was a picture under the text, which showed the dead body of a baby on a hospital bed; but not just any baby. It was one of the deformed creatures that we had seen earlier.

"Fuck, man." Torres said.

I scrolled down.

Day 27: Subject 3 has given birth to her baby via C-section. Just like Subject 3, Subject 1's baby displayed physical deformities and inability to breathe on its own. It was put inside an incubator, where it will continue to be monitored.

Day 31: Subject 3's baby has displayed signs of rapid growth, reaching the weight of 23 pounds (10kg) in just 4 days. It has also grown in size and has therefore been put inside a bigger incubator.

Day 40: The baby continues to grow, surpassing 8 feet in height and 396 lbs (225kg). That is not the only peculiar thing about it, however. Upon running a scan, it was revealed that the baby has its own baby growing inside the stomach. It has therefore been dubbed The Mother. The funds provided by the college are not sufficient anymore, but if I ask for more, they will require strong proof of why it's necessary. I have no doubt they would shut down the project if they saw what was going on here, but I can't stop now. So instead I'll use my own funds in secret.

Day 52: The Mother has already given birth to three other babies, each of them deformed even more than itself. It is still unable to breathe on its own and must therefore remain inside the incubator, but more and more fetuses seem to be forming inside of it.

Day 67: The Mother's babies have displayed the same patterns as her, giving birth to their own babies at a rapid pace. The babies, dubbed the Rejects can grow enormously, surpassing humans in size and physical prowess. When they're juvenile, their skin is as soft as ours, but as they grow, their skin toughens starting from the tips of their fingers and toes, until it reaches the area around the chest and heart. Once their skin has toughened completely, it becomes nearly impossible to kill them, however further tests are needed. Another peculiar thing is that the Mother seems to be able to communicate with her children, despite not having any visible form of communication. Either way, the project has been deemed a success and will therefore be shut down tomorrow, with everyone but the Mother terminated. The Mother will be sent to [REDACTED] for further study, where I will personally lead the testing.

Although the initial goal of the Fertility Project has been achieved, the results cannot be used with civilians for conception and will therefore instead be used as an arms trade on the black market. The assistant, subjects and participating students will be disposed of, to prevent any risks of sensitive data being leaked.

The document ended there.

"Well fuck me sideways. What a piece of shit." Torres said.

"Something must have gone wrong before they could terminate the project and the Rejects." I said "We have to check out the experiment downstairs."

I could see Torres' protests on his face, but he knew we had to do this. Bryans nodded as well and we wasted no time. I entered through the hole in the door first and my teammates followed. The basement stairwell was dark, illuminated only by our flashlights and the now dim glow of the PC monitor from the office. but as we got down, we reached yet another busted door, which emitted a greenish glow from inside. Carefully, we stepped inside and gasped in awe at the sight before us.

In front of us was a big room, very tall and very spacious and on each side of the room were long rows of giant incubators that looked like upright tubes, filled with green liquid. At the very end of the room stood a much larger incubator, at least three times the size of the other tubes. A behemoth of a creature was dormant inside, only visible as a silhouette from here. The Mother, I thought instantly. Each tube had lights inside, which gave off the sickly green glow, reflecting it on the walls and floor, even bathing me and my teammates in green.

A lot of the test-tubes had deformed, emaciated creatures of various sizes and shapes inside them, who looked to be dormant and unaware of our presence, but most of the tubes were empty, with broken glass and green liquid spilled out of them on the floor. I recognized the green-brown muck as the one we'd seen back at the entrance.

"Guess we now know what happened here." Bryans said.

"How the fuck did the college fund something like this, without knowing it was happening right under their noses?" Torres asked.

"You read the report." I interjected "Richards used his own funding, in addition to the college's. Let's check out that tube at the front. That might be the Mother."

We proceeded down the room, carefully observing the remaining intact tubes around us for any sudden movements. As we got closer, the Mother became more and more clear. A creature which easily towered over 12 feet despite being hunched over, its body was emaciated, except for the stomach, which bulged prominently. The arms were disproportionately long, almost reaching down to the creature's ankles. The face, despite having a breathing mask over its mouth, was clearly as deformed as that of its children, with a bulging, lumpy forehead and thin strands of long, black hair floating in the tube's green liquid. Her eyes were closed and even from here, the skin of the creature seemed thick and scaly, like a crocodile's. I knew there was no way we could kill this thing with bullets, so I hoped the C4 was enough to blow her into smithereens.

"Bryans, let's set up that bad boy and get the fuck out." Torres said.

Bryans gladly whipped out the C4 and placed it on the tube. Almost as soon the explosive touched the glass, the Mother opened her eyes, fixating her penetrating gaze on Bryans. And then the sound of glass breaking behind us filled the room. We turned around to see the creatures crawling out of their tubes, producing gurgling noises as the liquid poured out of their mouths. We instantly opened fire, mowing down the creatures that pathetically tried to crawl out of their tanks.

But then another sound of glass breaking occurred, this time from the Mother's tube. I turned around just in time to see the Mother firmly holding Torres by the torso like a toy, lifting him up with ease. By then, all her children in the room were already dead, so we focused our attention to the Mother, opening fire on her. As expected, the bullets simply bounced off and we watched in horror as Torres started screaming more and more, the Mother's grip on him tightening like a vice. We continued shooting relentlessly and for an instant, the Mother's grip on Torres loosened. And then she squeezed again, forcefully and quickly this time, crushing Torres' body and instantly killing him.

She threw his limp body across the room and she would have hit me (and probably crushed me with the impact), had I not evaded.

"Fall back!" I shouted to Bryans we started running for our lives.

A very deep, very loud groan resounded in the room, making the walls vibrate. We heard the sound of something wet and heavy slapping the ground and I turned around for a moment, enough to see the Mother feverishly crawling towards us on her palms, with a glint of pure hate in her eye. We ran back up the stairs and I went through the gap in the door first, turning around to see if Bryans was following me. He was just about to get out as well, when the boney hand of the Mother wrapped around him. He tried breaking free, but he must have realized he was done for, because right before he got dragged back down into the dark stairwell, he threw the C4 detonator to me.

"Go!" He shouted as he got pulled down.

I grabbed it and knew there was no point in trying to rescue him. I ran as fast as I could and then I heard the groan of the Mother once more, spurring me to run even faster. As soon as I was one step out of the building I detonated the explosive, causing an alarmingly loud bang inside the building. I kept running as I listened to the building crumbling behind me with a progressively louder noise, until it was almost deafening. Only when I was at a safe distance, I stopped and turned around to face my masterpiece of ruination.

The building was completely collapsed and all that remained was a pile of rubble and debris. I leaned on my knees, exhaling in relief. And then I heard something moving in the debris. I looked up and sure enough, there was something stirring under. In seconds, a giant, dust covered hand popped out, propping itself clumsily on the rubble. And then the other hand. The debris started shifting in large quantities and the head of the Mother slowly arose, groaning, now with such hate and anger that it looked like it could swallow the entire world. She made one step forward with her hand and then braced herself with the other, slowly, but surely pulling herself out of the rubble.

I raised my rifle, trying to aim for its eyes and just before I pulled the trigger, another deafening explosion occurred. I felt the heat of the blast even at this distance as the missile hit the Mother. She screamed in agony this time, but also recoiled in visible fear. Another missile and I heard someone shout 'Get to cover!'. I did as they ordered and as I turned around, I saw the APC which brought us here pull up and unload at the thing mercilessly. There were dozens of other APCs and even two tanks, from what I could see and they were all giving the Mother a barrage of missiles and bullets.

The Mother groaned and flailed her arms, as if trying to swat at pesky mosquitoes, but gradually her scaly skin had started to get bruised and then bloody. And then when her skin was soft enough, the armored infantry of the company ran in and started shooting at the weak spot at her chest. I joined in and fired at the creature with the anger of a man whose entire unit was gruesomely killed, not holding back. The Mother screamed and spun around, trying to retreat now, but her screams faded away and she miserably fell back on top of the debris, breathing out her last breath.

"Hold your fire!" Someone shouted.

Then, there was silence. A few armored security personnel hesitantly approached the dead giant and confirmed she was dead, before the commander started shouting various orders to his units on what to do next. When he was done, he approached me and asked:

"Where's the rest of your unit?"

"KIA." I responded "We didn't know what we were up against."

"And yet you're somehow still alive. Again." He said behind his helmet mockingly.

I didn't respond. He grunted and said:

"Mission complete. You did well. You should go back and report to HQ. Leave the cleanup to us, Survivor."

The Fertility Project

You may have asked yourself at least once in your life, if you could go back in time, what would you change? I never contemplated that question until recently and now I think about it every day, regret my decision to ever join that damned experiment. If I knew then what I knew now, I would have taken the pencil from Richards' desk and stabbed him in the neck over and over until he died. Jailtime would be a small price to pay for that. Let me take it from the top.

I work as an assistant in genetics at a college, which you may not have heard of before. Either way, to keep things safe, I won't disclose any important information, to protect myself and anyone else who may be somehow related to the matter.

Professor Richards was a prominent person in the college, adored by both students and his coworkers, for his dedication to work, extensive knowledge and ability to motivate his attendees to contribute in the lessons and outside of them. He often conducted projects here and there, small experiments to prove or debunk a theory or something else, and more often than not, he had a plethora of student-volunteers who were willing to do all the work for him. I rarely participated in any of the projects, save for when it really piqued my interest on a matter that I wanted to see the results on. Richards trusted me the most and always gave me the most sensitive tasks to perform, passing on his own knowledge onto me in the process.

More often than not, he was like a fatherly figure to me, rather than a superior. He could probably sense that I grew up without a father's love, so he stepped in to take me under his wing. Now when I look back, I start to realize that he probably never really cared, but needed someone that he could use for his twisted, insidious intentions.

It all started a few months ago when he invited me to his office with a proposal he was very excited about. "How would you like to be a part of history, Victor?" He asked me.

Of course I was always willing to take up big projects, especially if there was a chance for recognition, so I immediately answered 'yes'.

"Well, we have one big project upcoming." Richards said "The biggest one yet. If everything goes well with it, we'll be famous and rich. You'll never have to work as an assistant another day in your life!"

I asked him what this was about and he handed me a folder. When I opened it, I saw with big, bold letters the name *THE FERTILITY PROJECT*. In short, the documents described what the project would be about, who would participate and how long it would last. The purpose of the project was simple – find female test subjects that were unable to conceive children and artificially impregnate them. Aside from Richards and I, there would be twelve volunteering students from the college and five female test subjects.

I carefully reviewed the documents and saw that the project was funded by the college – not that I had any suspicions about Richards' authenticity at that time, anyway. He said that if I wanted to participate, I would have to sign an NDA and make sure not to tell anyone, under the threat of federal violation and long jail time. The same went for the students. If they told anyone about the project, including their family members, they risked getting kicked out of college and facing jailtime.

Although I disliked the idea of being chained down like that, at the time it seemed like a small price to pay for such greatness. I signed it and Richards whipped out two Cuban cigars.

"Been saving these for a special occasion. Doesn't get any more special than this." He said as he gave one to me and lit it up.

I was scheduled to meet Richards in the Biology and Genetics building in two days and when I arrived, I was surprised to see a guardhouse instead of a gate and a guard sitting inside. The college had somehow managed to set this up seemingly overnight. The guard asked for my name and I gave it to him, too confused and docile at the moment to refuse. The guard politely explained that with the upcoming project, the college had to hire a security company to keep things safe. He said there were five guards in total, each stationed in a separate part of the campus, with one guard being in the Biology building at all times.

I asked the guard if they knew what the project was about, but they seemed oblivious to it. All they knew was they had to keep the college grounds safe from any suspicious or violent activities. I gave him a courteous smile and left to meet Richards. When I arrived, another guard stood in front of Richards' office and stopped me from entering.

"It's okay, he's with me." Richards shouted and the guard let me through.

I went inside and all of the project participants were there, including the students and the five female subjects. The subjects were women between the ages of 20-28 and while Richards and I were permitted to go home at the end of the day, the students and subjects had to remain inside the building at all times.

"Professor Richards, we don't have adequate rooms for them to stay here." I said.

"Everything has been arranged." Richards said "The students will be staying on the second floor, while the subjects will be on the third floor. Since the project is so secretive, the guard is not permitted to leave the first floor. His job here will be to prevent anyone unwanted from entering the building or in the worst-case scenario, to stop students from leaving before the project is over. Unless they sign the paper to void the contract that is, in which case they would need to refund the college for the funds provided to the project. Trust me when I say, the funds are extremely high and you probably wouldn't want to do it. Now, let's show you all to your rooms."

My eyes widened when we went up to the second floor and I realized that two of the classrooms have been completely rearranged into unrecognizable rooms. Instead of chairs and desks, there were night tables and beds, giving off the impression of a dorm, rather than study building. The third floor was even stranger, with the classrooms not only being rearranged, but the entire floor seemingly renovated to instead have a row of five doors, which led into tiny cells. The women were each assigned to a cell and locked. It was explained that it was for their own safety, but should they want to drop out of the experiment at any given moment, they were free to do so – again, he emphasized the price they'd have to pay for such a choice.

I started getting a bad feeling by this point. None of this seemed right and no matter how many times Richards' uttered the word 'voluntary', nothing seemed so about this. The students and the women seemed very enthusiastic however, and were hanging on every word the professor said, obeying orders without questions.

On the first day, the crew went to the lab and created a solution, which was put into vials and injected into the subjects. Each student had his own role, ranging from performing subject check-ups, preparing food for the project members, taking blood samples, etc. My duty was to oversee the entire situation and assist if necessary, while providing medical help in case of an emergency. At around 3pm, all initial tests have been completed, so Richards instructed the students to go back to their dorm rooms, while he told me to follow him into his office.

He sat by his computer, a wide grin on his face at the satisfaction of a job well done for the day.

"I'll have one task for you, Victor." He said "You may go home whenever you want, but what I may need your help with is monitoring the subjects. Come here."

He gestured and I went around his table to look at the PC screen. On the screen were five camera feeds, monitoring the subjects' cells.

"I'll be sleeping in the office." He said "But if something comes up for me, I will need you to monitor the subjects."

It sounded like an order, not a request.

"Sure, professor. You can count on me." I said, trying to hide my uncertainty.

"Alright. Well, that's it for the first day. You can go home now, get some rest. We have a lot of work ahead of us tomorrow."

For days, nothing changed and the crew performed their regular duties during the day. And then about a week later, Subjects 2 and 4 started to complain about the extreme isolation they were subjected to. They asked to be let out, but Richards outright refused, reminding them about the cost they would need to pay. Despite that, Subject 2 protested, so Richards ordered one of the students to sedate her. He did as instructed and the subject fell asleep. It was around 8 pm when I went into Richards' office to report the day's findings and I realized that Subject 2 was still asleep.

"Professor Richards, the subject should not be asleep for that long." I said.

"She shouldn't." He said "But she's not sleeping. She's been euthanized."

My eyes widened in horror.

"What did you say?" I asked.

"We couldn't risk letting her out. The student doesn't know what he did, so let's keep it that way. We don't want him wracking himself with guilt.

"Are you out of your mind?! You killed her?!" I raised my voice, to which he gave me a stern look.

"Know your place, boy." He said "This project is the most important thing we'll ever work on. We can't let it go to waste because some nobody decided to opt out of it and disclose secret information."

"You can't be serious!" I shouted.

"I am." He said "And subject 4 has been complaining as well. I am going to need you to euthanize her."

"That's out of the question!"

We had a heated discussion and I told him I'll be leaving the project and reporting him to the police, when he whipped out the papers and showed them to me. He pointed to the section which showed that I agreed to be part of the project until it was finished and that if there came to any misconduct, all participants would be treated as equally guilty.

"You son of a bitch!" I said.

He simply smirked and told me to do my job, handing me the injection. I hesitated for a long time, but in the end, I had to do it. I was afraid of going to prison so much that I didn't care if I had to end someone else's life. That doesn't take away from the fact that I felt extremely guilty giving the patient an injection, while lying to her face that she'd be back to her husband tomorrow by noon. Richards even made me dispose of the bodies and made me agree on a story with him to tell to the students, that the subjects were released in the middle of the night.

I agreed to everything he said, feeling sick to my stomach. He told me to go home and take the next day off. I did as he commanded and needless to say, got no sleep that night. I battled with myself the entire next day on whether I should go to the authorities, but again, I was too selfish and afraid for myself to do so. When I returned to work the following day, I found Richards and the students in one of the classrooms, ecstatic. When I asked what was going on, Richards said:

"Victor, we did it. Subjects 1 and 3 are pregnant. This is a huge breakthrough in science."

My jaw dropped. I honestly haven't even thought about the potential success of the project, so I was surprised, to say the least. I'd be lying if I said I wasn't excited, myself. This was indeed a breakthrough in science. We wasted no time performing check-ups on the subjects, taking blood samples, etc.

Over the next few days, the subjects' weights have been increasing rapidly and their stomachs have grown in size. Ultrasound displayed the growth of the fetus at an abnormal rate and we started to get a little worried, since the size which we had seen by then was not supposed to be visible by the first trimester, let alone after just three weeks. Richards ordered us to carefully monitor the subjects, in case their health starts to slip up.

And then came the worst day that I experienced during the project. It was day 26, I remember distinctly, and Subject 1 was complaining about the severe pain in her stomach. I examined her and the baby was kicking with extreme force, so much that I could see the bulges from the impact on the subject's stomach. I begged Richards to take the subject to a hospital, but he wouldn't hear it. He told me to give her some painkillers and get back into his office. By this time the students were already asleep in their rooms and since the cells on the third floor were soundproof, not even the subjects from adjacent cells heard the woman screaming, let alone anyone else. Richards and I observed Subject 1 on camera, as she writhed in pain. She banged on the floor, begging to be let out, after which she lay on the bed, holding her stomach and screaming in pure agony. I saw her stomach stretching out, as if something poked it from the inside and then her skin ripped open and a tiny hand emerged. Blood sprayed out like a fountain and I saw a deformed, blood-covered head pop out, further opening the abdomen.

The subject screamed, now more in terror than pain, as she helplessly watched her baby burst through her stomach. Only seconds later, her head dropped onto the bed and she stopped moving. The baby started crying, but it was a kind of cry I had never heard before. It sounded guttural and gurgling.

"Victor, what are you waiting for?!" Richards yelled "Go take care of the baby!"

I stared at the thing on the camera, unable to move. Whatever that thing was, it wasn't human. It had an abnormally large head, extremities of unequal proportions and a voice that sounded anything but human. It cried vigorously for a while, gradually losing its potency and going completely silent.

"Victor!" Richards yelled again, but I was frozen in place.

Richards violently stood up and stormed out of his office. I saw on the cameras that he was entering cell one. I came to my senses and figured that I had to insure myself somehow, or stop the project. I browsed Richards' desktop and found the folder containing the details of the project. I glanced at the camera and realized that Richards was examining the dead baby and mother. I entered his email and sent all the details of the project to my email, nervously tapping on the desk as the files transferred. Richards was done wrapping the bodies in a sheet and started coming back, so as soon as the email was sent, I deleted the sent mail and returned to the camera feed, stepping away from the PC.

Richards burst inside, beads of sweat forming on his temples.

"Are they dead?" I asked.

"Of course they're dead, you idiot! I should report you to the project stakeholders for insubordination!"

"Excuse me?"

"If you had arrived in time, the baby of the subject could have survived!"

"That's not true! I'm not even trained to handle this sort of situation!"

Richards sat in his chair and exhaled deeply, rubbing his eyes.

"The bodies are wrapped up. Take them into the basement." He said sternly.

I dreaded the idea of carrying around a dead mother and her infant, but I didn't want to defy the professor right now, to avoid arousing suspicion. I hauled the bodies downstairs and returned to Richards' office, who still seemed pretty pissed.

"Go home." He said, staring at the screen of his computer.

"Professor, if you need help I can-"

"Leave!"

He didn't need to tell me again. I wished him a good night and left, still shaking. As soon as I got home, I downloaded the contents of the email and deleted any remaining evidence. I could use this somehow, but I was too tired and traumatized to think of a plan. I went to bed, the events of the night replaying in my head. That night I kept having recurring nightmares of deformed, monstrous toddlers chasing me. When I woke up, I found the reality to be barely better than the haunting nightmares, but I had to go back to work. I knew Richards had me by the balls and I had no choice but to comply with his demands.

When I arrived, the students were going about their normal everyday activities. Richards explained that he lied to the students and told them Subject 1 had to be taken to the hospital due to complications. I was appalled by his actions, but then remembered that I'm not that much different, so I stopped myself from judging him too much. Out of the five subjects, only two remained – Subject 3 and Subject 5. Subject 5 still showed no response to the treatment and Subject 3's stomach kept growing rapidly. And then just two days after the death of Subject 1, she gave birth.

Richards was ready this time, having invested in an incubator and he delivered the baby himself. The baby was just as deformed as the one from Subject 1. Richards separated the mother and the baby without even letting her take a look at her child, much to her protests. He ordered us to close the cell as he took the baby out. We had no choice but to comply, even the students, who reluctantly followed his orders. Subject 3 cried for hours, but Richards muted the camera and focused on observing the baby in the incubator. Ten days later, the baby had grown in size enormously, reaching above 8 feet in height and over 390 pounds. It had grown long extremities, its skin had become extremely hard, so needles could no longer penetrate it and its face no longer resembled that of a human, with various lumps and visible deformities on it. That wasn't the only thing, though. A scan revealed that the creature itself had babies growing inside of it, at a seemingly fast pace, just like babies of the subjects. Due to this, Richards dubbed the creature the Mother.

The incubator could no longer sustain a creature of such a size and I knew Richards could not possibly ask the college for more funds. I also knew he would not risk revealing the details of the project to the stakeholders, as they would shut it down immediately.

He told me to take some time off and that he would let me know when my services were needed again. This was bad, because I knew he was up to no good, so to occupy myself during the sleepless nights, I reviewed the project documents that I had stolen. Sure enough, ten days later Richards told me to resume my duties. When I arrived, I saw an electronic door, which hadn't been there before, in his office behind his computer. It led downstairs into a basement, which was expanded onto a huge area that resembled a laboratory.

There were enormous test tubes filled with green liquid all over the place, with the biggest one being at the far end of the room. The Mother was there, now much bigger than I remembered it to be, seemingly sleeping and although its stomach was bulging, I could see more, smaller deformed creatures in nearby incubators. Richards filled me in on the details:

"The Mother gave birth to three of them and continues to create more. The scan showed two more babies inside her stomach. In addition to that, it would seem that its babies also carry their own babies. They are extremely sick though, so I have dubbed them the Rejects."

"The college approved this?" I asked.

"Of course not. They don't know about this. I used my own funding to further the research."

I realized then that there were only nine students present in the building.

"Where are the other participants?" I asked.

Richards paused before answering:

"They were found dead in their rooms. Suicide. The weaklings couldn't live with the knowledge of what had to be done for greatness."

I also realized that Subject 3 was gone. I didn't ask him where she was, nor how he disposed of the bodies. That left us with only Subject 5 remaining. She was extremely malnourished and sick, as Richards saw no use in feeding or taking care of her. Over the course of next few days, fewer and fewer students kept showing up. More committed suicide, whereas a lot of them were killed handling the babies. It soon became apparent that the creatures were toughening up quickly, their skin becoming hard, their speed and strength increasing way above humans', etc. Richards had one of the grown versions placed inside the cell of the previous subjects and sent one student to feed the creature. The creature was highly aggressive, so by the time it was done with the student, what was left of him was strewn all over the cell.

Everyone was fully aware of Richards' intentions by then, but no one dared oppose him. A lifetime in prison put anyone off from trying anything stupid, like reporting him to the authorities. Every day he would emphasize multiple times how we would be rich by the time we were done, or how everyone would end up in prison for life, if anyone decided to betray him. He knew exactly what to say to instill fear in his subordinates, including me.

Out of all project participants, only Richards, myself and three more students remained by day 60 and I knew it was only a matter of time until it was my turn. Things were getting out of hand and I knew I had to put a stop to this.

Richards never let anyone down in the lab without his permission and he was the sole holder of the keycard which opened the electronic lock, but that was of no interest to me. I had to get Subject 5 and the students out of there. Based on the conversations I've had with the guards, they were loyal to their company and not to Richards, so I knew I could trust them with some of the details. I scheduled my email containing all the project data to automatically be sent to the security company and the college twelve hours after I start my shift. I then pulled the guard from my building aside. I told him everything about the project and how most of the people were dead now, to which he seemed surprised and terrified. He agreed to wait until Richards went to sleep in his room and that we would then unlock the cell and let everyone out. Before we managed to finalize our plan though, Richards called me into his office, interrupting us. I followed him there and stood in front of his desk, as he stared at the computer screen for a while. When he decided it was time to pay attention to me, he looked at me and said:

"Victor. How are you feeling?"

"I'm fine, professor." I lied.

"No, you're not. I can see it on you. This whole thing bothers you. I know it."

"It doesn't. I'm okay with this."

"Victor. You're a horrible liar. But I have something that might change your mind. Come with me."

He opened the electronic door and led me downstairs. By now, most of the incubators had deformed creatures of various sizes inside of them, some of them much taller than humans, others the size of toddlers. Richards led me around and stopped in front of one of the incubators.

"Look." He pointed and my eyes widened.

Inside the test tube was a very small, perfectly healthy, perfectly normal human baby.

"Given birth to by one of these monstrosities." He said "You see? We achieved greatness."

"How is this possible?"

"I believe there's a variety of factors. According to all the data I've gathered, there is a very, very small chance of a normal human baby being born, but there *is* a chance."

"But that means the project is a failure. We would need to breed dozens, if not hundreds of these creatures, in hopes of getting one healthy baby."

"No! It is *not* a failure!" He rebuked "We're going to go down in history, why can't you see this?"

"I'm sorry professor, but the only thing you'll be remembered as will be a cold, heartless murderer who pretended to be a scientist. I know what the project is truly about. I've read your files and I know you never intended to use the project for any so-called greatness. All you wanted was to make money and this gives you a chance to sell these creatures as a weapon on the black market. And I also know that dropping out of the project never posed any threat to the participants. You lied to us."

"That's not-"

"I've already contacted the security agency and the college. They will know everything soon enough."

"How dare you!" He scoffed, before calming down "Well, no matter."

He pulled out a pistol from behind his back and pointed it at me.

"The subject is a success and the Mother will be transferred to a new base for further research. I planned on killing off the students and the remaining subject tonight and offering you a chance to come with me, but since you know too much, you'll have to join them."

"You can kill me, but you won't get away with what you've done. You can't stop this, professor."

Just then, there was a sound of glass cracking behind Richards. He turned around in time to see one of the test tubes breaking, the green liquid pouring out. The creature inside stumbled out, voraciously gurgling and striding towards the professor.

"Stay back!" Richards fired a few shots into the creature, but it only flinched.

And then the Mother opened her eyes. Her eyes were completely black and yet despite that, I knew that her gaze was fixed directly on me. She groaned, emitting a deep vibration and her children raised her heads in response. More tubes broke and before I knew it, the professor and I were running back upstairs, Richards locking the doors with his keycard. There was a loud banging and I turned around just enough to see a dent appear on the door. When we reached his office, Richards fumbled for his computer, frantically clicking.

"No, I can't let my data get destroyed!" He said to no one in particular.

The loud bang now resounded directly on the door behind Richards, but he seemed oblivious to it. I didn't stay to see what would happen to him. I ran the hell out as the bangs got louder, just in time to hear the door break and a cacophony of gunshots and monstrous screams ensue. Richards screamed in agony, before his own voice got drowned out. The guard was there and had a visibly confused look on his face.

"No time, we gotta save the others!" I shouted.

"No, there's no time!" He grabbed me by the arm. The screams of those creatures resounded behind us and I could see them emerging from Richards' office, covered in blood, with blood-thirsty looks on their faces. I stood there for a moment contemplating my next action, but my cowardice took hold once more and I knew that I wouldn't be able to make it if I went for the others. So instead, I listened to the guard and we both bolted out of there.

"Go, go! Intervention will be here soon!" The guard shouted as we ran, but only moments later, I heard him get grabbed, as the monsters piled on top of him and ripped him into pieces.

I ran outside and stopped only when I reached the gate. The guard who was there stopped me and upon recognizing me, said that he was informed of the situation of the project. When I told him that there's been an outbreak, his eyes widened and told me to stay here, while he investigates. I begged him not to go, mostly because I didn't want to be left alone, but my pleas fell on deaf ears and he scurried off.

I went inside the guardhouse and picked up the phone, only just then realizing that I had blood on my clothes. I had no idea how I had gotten it on me, but upon inspection, I realized it wasn't mine. I tried dialing 911, but there was no signal. Upon reading the guideline on the side, I realized that the phone only took calls, but couldn't make them. I dropped the handset when I looked at the camera feed and saw one of the guards getting jumped by those creatures and getting ripped into pieces.

They were everywhere and most of the guards were dead.

I couldn't stay there, or I'd die. I went out of the guardhouse and ran towards the wooded area, looking behind every now and again to make sure nothing was following me. After what felt like forever and my legs started to give way, I stopped to take a break. The campus was far behind me and no one followed me. From there, I made my way safely home.

Out of all the participants of the Fertility Project, I was the only confirmed survivor later on. I have no idea what exactly happened, but I heard that the biology building had a pipe explosion, which caused the entire place to come down. Whether it was that, or something else, I'm glad, because it hopefully killed The Mother and her nasty children.

I wake up every night, seeing her black, penetrating gaze through the test-tube and I feel as if she knows where I am at all times, despite not seeing me. The guilt of letting those poor students and subjects die wracks me every day, as well. I don't feel sorry for the human baby that most likely got killed, though. Nothing good could have come out of those monsters. The only consolation I have is the fact that Richards died before he could fully weaponize and sell his project. The authorities are after me now and I don't know if they intend to sentence me to a life in prison, but I'll make it easy for them.

There's a gun next to me and when I'm done writing this, I'm going to use it. Hopefully, I'll be able to sleep peacefully again, for the first time in many months.

The morgue

The ad itself made me shiver, but at the same time it was appealing. It said:

Earn 120$ per night as a night guard in the morgue. Apply now!

I'd been jobless for a while and had to afford to pay my rent and late bills and with this kind of pay I'd be able to live like a king. So I applied hesitantly, half-hoping I wouldn't get a response from the company. Not even two hours later, I got an email from the employer:

Thank you for applying to our position of night guard in morgue. We are happy to inform you that your skills are suitable for our company and would hereby like to offer you a one year contract.

If you agree to the terms, please leave your signature via the online signature website listed below and be at [REDACTED] by 10 pm tonight.

You will receive a payment of 600$ weekly on the provided bank account.

Tonight? I thought it was a little too soon, but I didn't complain. I didn't know what to expect or who I'd meet there, so I put on my shirt and jeans and went to the address a little early.

I was there at 9:40 pm and a middle-aged man who seemed to be a morgue worker greeted me.

"Hi. Ethan, right? I'm George." He shook my hand with a smile "I know you were probably sent here on short notice, but the security company whose services we employ was in need of a new guard for tonight's shift right away."

"So I'm outsourced from a security company to your morgue?" I asked.

"That's right. You work for an outsourcing security company and from what I hear, they pay pretty well. So who knows, you may get an even better position in the future." He winked.

"Right. So about the duties here…" I started.

"Oh, that. No big deal, just make sure no one breaks in." He leaned in and said "Or out."

We stared at each other for a moment, but then he chuckled and said:

"I'm just kidding. Well listen, my shift is over, so I'll be going now. Just sit tight in the office and relax until 6 am. That's when the first shift arrives here."

And with that he left. I sat down by the desk in the office. I thought this probably isn't going to be so bad. There was a paper in front of me and after observing it, I realized it was a list or rules addressed to me. It said:

To the new guard,

Welcome to The Company. Below is the list of rules for your job:

1. The first thing you should do is conduct a full sweep of the area to make sure nothing is out of the ordinary (including the crypt). Important note: if any of the body chambers are pulled out in the crypt, push them back in. They should remain pushed in at all times.

2. After the sweep you may remain in the office until the end of the shift.

There were more rules listed below, but I decided to first check the place out. It was fairly small, with one big room that had medical supplies in it, the crypt and a bathroom. I first decided to get the worst out of the way – the crypt.

I left the office and opened the sturdy crypt door, immediately getting hit by a wave of cold air. Inside were two body carts in the middle of the room and cold chambers on the walls. All of them were closed, so I hastily left the room. On my way back from the bathroom, I saw a man in a lab coat standing in the medical room. He was fiddling with some of the tools next to a body bag.

"Jesus, you scared the hell out of me." I said.

He shot me a bemused glance and continued working.

"I thought everyone left already. My name's Ethan, I'm the new guard." I said but again, he simply ignored me.

I waved my hand in dismissal and returned to the office. I was about to continue reading the rules, when there was a sudden creaking sound reverberating throughout the building. It was faint, but it sounded like the pipes. It intermittently lasted for a few seconds and paused just as long. I ignored it and slacked some more, checking my phone. But the longer the creaking lasted though, the more I got unnerved, because they sounded less like pipes and more like... moans.

I got out to ask the employee about that, but he had already gone home by then. I couldn't tell where exactly the sound was coming from, but it sounded like the crypt, so I went there. As soon as I opened the door, the whole building went silent. I held my breath as I observed the room and then realized that one of the body drawers was pulled out slightly. I pushed it back in and bolted back to the office. The creaking was completely gone by then. I continued reading:

3. *You may sleep in the office, but it is inadvisable*

Just then, the loudest sound just about made me jump out of my skin.

"PLEASE! SOMEONE LET ME OUT!" The voice cried from somewhere and the pipes carried his voice. I stood up, heart racing.

"LET ME OUT, I CAN'T BREATHE!" The voice repeated, now followed by a series of loud bangs. I opened the office door and the screams were apparently coming from the crypt. I shuddered, but decided to open the door.

"I'M NOT DEAD, THIS IS A MISTAKE! SOMEONE!" The voice got louder as soon as I opened the sturdy door.

"Where are you?!" I frantically looked around, while the man continued screaming bloody murder and banging.

I approached the source of the sound and leaned in to listen and make sure that this was the right chamber.

"I'M NOT DEAD! LET ME OUT! PLE-"

The voice and the banging suddenly stopped when I abruptly pulled out the drawer and was met with a cold, dead body of a middle-aged man. I stood there, staring at the corpse, my mind unable to comprehend what just happened. I heard it very clearly, felt the banging as I held the drawer handle and then it was as if someone just shut it off abruptly. Was my mind playing tricks on me?

I pushed the drawer back in and bolted out of there, shutting the office door and thinking that applying here may have been a bad idea. I felt like I was on needles, but convinced myself after a while that it was all in my head. I continued reading the rules:

4. You may play music to kill the silence, so long as it doesn't drown out any outside noises

---

5. If you hear incoherent sounds coming from the crypt, you can ignore them.
6. If those sounds turn into panicked screams, do the following: 1) if the screams are female, ignore them until they stop. Do not enter the crypt during this time under any circumstances 2) if the screams are male, locate the source of the screams and pull out the body drawer. This should stop the screaming.

The page ended there. I placed the paper down and leaned back in the chair. It was 1 am. I started feeling sleepy. After a while, my eyes started to shut. Just as I started drifting into dream, I felt a firm grip from behind on my shoulder. I instantly shot up, knocking the chair down in the process. No one was there.
I no longer felt sleepy. Everything was quiet for a while and I went to the bathroom once more. When I returned, it was 4 am and I was pretty much ready to end the shift here. I started thinking how it wasn't so bad for 120$, until I flipped the paper with the rules and realized there was something else written on the back:

7. All the staff will be out of the building by 10 pm, so if you see a man in a lab coat during your shift, DO NOT under any circumstances try to talk to him.

I reread the rule five times over, but the text remained the same. There was a gentle knock on the office door. I looked up and through the glass I saw the man in the lab coat grinning at me.
It's 4:30 now and he keeps knocking.

The hotel

A year ago, I decided to go on a trip for the weekend. Work was particularly stressful and my free time was pretty much nonexistent, so I figured I should take a few days off, away from the incessant emails and messages from the office.

I'm not exactly high demand when it comes to vacations and usually all I need is a little bit of time away from technology combined with a nice hiking trail. So I chose a town on top of the mountain South of where I live, since I figured two days there would be enough to refresh me.

The drive over there was long and tedious, but with occasional nice views here and there. It took me about 4 hours to get to the mountain itself and despite it being pitch black on the road, I could tell I was there due to the air becoming progressively colder. I wasn't even sure if I was in the right place until I turned on my GPS. At first my route was marked as 2 hours away, but then suddenly changed to 30 minutes away from the hotel I booked. Confused, because I was sure that it would take me at least 2 more hours to reach the destination, I just figured I miscalculated, or the GPS found a quicker route.

Hell, even when I reached the town I wasn't sure if I was in the right place, since the lights were mostly out and I could only see as far as my headlights illuminated in front of me. I didn't stop until the "you've arrived at your destination" notification sounded from the GPS and I saw that I was in front of an average-looking building. I looked at my GPS, but it showed the map as no landmarks around whatsoever. No hotel name, no streets, nothing. I chalked it up to bad signal and took another look at the building in front. I could tell it sort of looked like the hotel I booked, but I contemplated the fact that it looked nothing like in the pictures I saw.

Too tired from the drive to care, I parked my car, grabbed my things and went inside. The interior seemed pleasant enough, albeit a bit claustrophobic due to the narrow corridors.

"Hi." I smiled to the lady at the reception "I have a reservation."

"Yes, you're on the list. Welcome. Please sign here and I will show you to your room." The lady went from a I'm-dying-of-boredom state to perky.

I signed the papers and was escorted to my room on the 4th floor. The room itself looked quite luxurious, contrasting the exterior of the hotel.

"If you need anything, there's always someone at the reception." The clerk smiled again and left.

I looked outside the window, trying to take in the view, but it was pointless. Everything surrounding the outside of the hotel was pitch black. Not giving it a second thought, I slumped down on the bed and decided to sleep, not even setting an alarm for the first time in years. I was determined to sleep until my back started to hurt.

At some point during the night, I could hear some sounds coming from outside my room. It sounded like footsteps and giggling. I unlocked my cellphone and squinted, seeing it was 4:30am. What the hell were kids doing playing at this hour? Disregarding it, I went back to sleep. Just as I starter to doze off, I was startled awake by a loud bang outside my room. I opened my eyes, wide awake, staring through the darkness at the coat hanger in front of the door, which I could barely make out. I held my breath, trying to hear any more sounds, half-lazy and half-scared to get up and check out what that bang was.

I heard a muffled giggle again, starting to get annoyed at this point. Still, I continued staring at the coat hanger, ready to get up and tell the kids off if they continued. About two minutes passed and nothing happened. I sighed in relief and closed my eyes again. But for some reason I had this nagging feeling which I couldn't let go. I felt tense, unnerved even. I opened my eyes again and looked towards the coat hanger. Nothing. Just my imagination.

And it was then that I remembered something that sent cold shivers down my spine. There was no coat hanger when I arrived. I moved my gaze to my left very slowly and saw that my jacket was on the chair. I frantically looked back at the coat hanger, heart thumping in my chest.

That was no hanger. It was a fucking person. What I mistook as the top of the hanger was actually a face – a wide-eyed, grinning, toothy face – and it was staring right at me. I didn't dare to move. I was so petrified with fear that I could only hear the deafeningly loud and fast beat of my heart. And then I heard that giggle again. Muffled, sounding almost like it wasn't even coming from the room, but it unmistakably came from that creatures mouth.

I just laid there as that thing started moving across the room toward the window on my left. I could see its full form now. The head was round and maintained that blood-freezing grin the entire time and it stood unnaturally on a very thin and long body. The creature itself was in fact so tall, that it bent its knees and hunched its bony back forward when walking, making every step ever so slowly, letting its pale arms hang on the sides.

After what seemed like an eternity, it reached the window and stopped there, staring outside and letting out another giggle. I could see its reflection on the glass, which seemed to be frozen in place. Still grinning, still wide-eyed, just standing, staring in one spot. I knew I had to get out. It was now or never. Slowly, very slowly I started getting ready to jump out of bed, not taking my eyes off the creature for one second. I held my breath, moving my legs towards the edge and preparing to boost myself with my hands. And then the creature let out another muffled giggle which froze me in my place.

This one was different. It was longer, deeper, more guttural. And as the creature giggled, it slowly moved its head slightly to the left with an unnatural creaking sound, moving its gaze along with it. The reflection in the window stopped its movement the moment its gaze turned directly to me and as it did, the giggling suddenly stopped as well. It was just dead silence and my gaze meeting this thing's, neither of us blinking. It was all I could take. My survival instincts kicked in and I burst out of the room, hearing that creature giggling more maliciously now, almost like a hyena. As I ran through the hotel, I couldn't help but notice that the entire interior was now old, decayed and covered in dust. There were no lights anywhere. It's as if I was in a completely different building.

I didn't stop when I was out of that fucked up place. I didn't stop when I reached my car. I didn't stop until morning when the adrenaline finally subsided. On my way back, my GPS was going haywire so I stopped at a gas station to ask for directions. What the employee there told me shook me to the core.

When I told him that I came from that town and was looking for a way home, he shook his said and told me that I must be mistaken, since the town which was intended to be my original destination for vacation was at least three more hours away from where I stayed the night.

He said that there had been a small hotel there before, but it closed down due to unknown reasons around 20 years ago and had been abandoned ever since.

I never fully understood what happened that night and I haven't been able to make myself look it up. When my friends and coworkers talk about having a vacation in that same town, I just pretend I don't know the place well since it was a long time ago, even though they can tell something is wrong.

That was over one year ago and I haven't taken any vacations since then, save for days off when I just stay home. I can't sleep without the lights on anymore and sometimes, in the middle of the night I wake up with a rapid heart rate to the one sound that haunts me incessantly.

The same, slow, muffled giggle from the hotel.

The residential building

I come from a country where security guards aren't even registered as employees and are without proper training. Given the fact that I wasn't registered as an actual employee in my company, it was very easy to get fired depending on the boss's mood. And because he was able to slip past the law, he could also get away with paying his guards under minimum wage. If you don't like it - tough luck, there's someone else who will gladly jump in for that money. Not for this company, though. This company paid handsomely and took care of its employees as best it could, despite the pervasive dangers.

But before I get on my high horse, I'm here to tell you about why I quit my job. I used to work in a building as a regular night guard - which was a fancy way of being called an errand boy or gate boy.

Allow me to explain. My job was basically to open the gate for the residents of the building to let them in and out and keep an eye out for any suspicious activity on the monitors. But when the residents complained about us being overpaid for the work we do, we had to start doing maintenance jobs, which later turned into personal errands for arrogant old people.

All for the same pay, of course.

Back then I was too lazy and too tired from night shifts to start looking for another job, plus the company paid well, like I mentioned before, so I just settled for the one I had. Besides me there were three other guards - Dandelion (yes, his name literally translates to that), an economy graduate who kept boasting about his diploma on every occasion, especially to new residents, until he would be reminded to open the gate. Besides him there was Robert, a middle aged divorced man that lived with his mother. He was always surprisingly kind to his coworkers, but over the phone we would hear him yelling at his sister in Hungarian when he was frustrated. George, who was ex military and was now retired was the last one. Smart and humorous, his right eye always half-shut due to a condition he had made us feel uneasy whenever we saw him drive off. We mostly had rotations, 12 hours day shift, 12 hours night and then two days off, which messed up our sleep. I needed the cash back then, so I volunteered for night shifts whenever I could. Now, the building itself has always been pretty calm, save for the incessant complaints of the tenants about their TVs not working, the key not fitting into their lock anymore or someone parking in their spot.

I spent most of the nights watching movies on my laptop or sleeping, due to the lack of activity during nights. In my year of working there, there have been only a couple of times that tenants needed something after midnight, and most of the time it was something they could easily handle themselves, but since they got used to being pampered, I had no choice but to check it out.

That brings us to the fateful night which resulted in me quitting the job. It was an ordinary night and I replaced Dandelion, who as usually, had a smartass remark to share before leaving.

"So then I told him," He said "I ain't gonna check out the basement at night if you don't fix the lights down there."

He was one of those guys you must have met at least once in your life - the guy in the circle of friends that always shares stories about his triumphs and genius remarks and never being the loser in any situation, whether it's something petty or important. As usually, I dismissed his remark and told him to go get some rest, too irritated to listen to his smartmouthing.

I sat down and checked what he wrote in the report book - Mrs Amstadt complained about a smell coming from her floor, nothing unusual found. That bitch seemed to be complaining about things all the time, mostly just to keep us occupied, I think. Placing my phone and laptop on the table, I browsed online for an interesting movie to watch.

The shift was going smoothly and I passed the time alongside some zombie flick, glancing at the monitors from time to time, just to make sure there was no one there. The only kind of activity I got thus far was a bunch of teens who sat in the vicinity of the camera and drank from a brown bag. Naturally, I had to chase them away and they never gave me any trouble for it. It was around 1 AM when the office phone rang. When I picked it up, there was nothing but static. After a few 'hellos' I hung up, concluding that it must have been old Peter the groundskeeper, who constantly had problems with his line.

"If you want something, come down here you lazy old shit." I rubbed my eyed, starting to feel sleepy. But the sound of weak and steady knocking on the door startled me wide awake. Through the glass on the door I was able to see Mr Markovic's pale skull-like face.

Cold sweat came all over me until I regained my composure and opened the door.

"What can I do for you, Mr Markovic?" I tried to sound polite unsuccessfully.

"Come with me, please." He grabbed me by the arm too firmly for a man his age.

"What can I help you with, sir?" I followed him, trying to pull away from his grip subtly, but unsuccessfully.

He mumbled something along the line of "this way, the time has come", but I didn't understand it back then. Whenever I tried asking him a question about what's wrong, he would ignore me and just keep pulling me by my arm. I wanted nothing more than to push this old man and see his frail body break into pieces on the floor, but decided to indulge in his request for the sake of my job. He took me to the elevator and then suddenly let me go. My arm was pulsating on the spot where he was clutching me.

"Third floor, sir?" I got no response again and he continued looking straight, not showing any signs of hearing what I said.

So I pushed number 3 and waited until the elevator stopped.

"Alright, let's see what the problem is Mr Markovic." I flew out of the elevator with him following closely behind me.

As we were nearing his room, 306, I could hear something that sounded like weeping. I stopped to listen.

"Is that your wife?" I asked him, but got no response again.

He kept looking at me very creepily from behind, but again not showing any signs of responsiveness. I moved towards room 306 and saw that the door was ajar. The weeping was now louder, so I carefully pushed the door open, partially illuminating the apartment hallway with the light from the corridor.

"Mrs Markovic?" I pointed my flashlight towards the elderly woman who was kneeling next to a couch, bawling her eyes out.

I couldn't see what she would be doing in a dark apartment, but I was starting to freak out by that point.

"He's gone he's gone he's gone" She chanted between tears "He to-told me he would be gone soon, but I-I didn't listen."

"Who's gone, Mrs Markovic?" I slowly entered the hallway, illuminating the back of the couch.

"My hu-husband. My de-dear husband. He's gone, he's gone."

"What are you talking about, Mrs Markovic, your husband is right he-"

I turned around, pointing the flashlight at the door but no one was there. The corridor stood dimly illuminated, but empty. I peeked out the door left and right and saw that it was empty, as well.

"Mr Markovic?" I called out and as I did, the hairs at the back of my neck stood up.

I returned into the apartment and slowly, very slowly
went around the chair. With one jerky motion I
illuminated the couch with my flashlight and I knew,
I just knew what I would see there. In the chair was
Mr Markovic's limp body, mouth agape, eyes looking
up in shock. He was still clutching the sides of the
chair firmly. Ignoring Mrs Markovic's weeping, I
pulled up my sleeve and pointed the flashlight to my
arm - the arm that Mr Markovic firmly held.
Above the elbow on the inside, there was a very
distinct bruise the size of a thumb. I didn't wait for the
my shift to end. Hell, I didn't even wait for the
ambulance to arrive. I got out of there as fast as I
could, sending a text to my boss that I quit and that he
can keep the final month's pay. The guys from work
said that after reviewing the footage they didn't see
Mr Markovic anywhere outside. They only saw me
leaving the office alone and going into the elevator.
It's been a year, but the bruise on my arm is still here.
In fact, maybe it's my imagination, but it seems to be
getting bigger.

Final notes

The book is over, but the guard has more tales to tell…

YOUR SAFETY IS OUR SUCCESS

Made in the USA
San Bernardino, CA
21 January 2020